Frank Barrett

The Harding Scandal

Volume 2

Frank Barrett

The Harding Scandal
Volume 2

ISBN/EAN: 9783337403720

Printed in Europe, USA, Canada, Australia, Japan

Cover: Foto ©Andreas Hilbeck / pixelio.de

More available books at **www.hansebooks.com**

THE HARDING SCANDAL

BY

FRANK BARRETT

AUTHOR OF

'THE ADMIRABLE LADY BIDDY FANE,' 'FETTERED FOR LIFE,' ETC.

IN TWO VOLUMES

VOL. II.

LONDON

CHATTO & WINDUS, PICCADILLY

1896

CONTENTS OF VOL. II.

CHAPTER XVI.

A NEW LEAD.

THE General's composition was not such stuff as stage villains are made of; he was not wicked from a diabolical love of wickedness. On the contrary, he would have very much preferred to steer clear of dangerous practices—to be benevolent, charitable, and worthily beloved by all ; in other words, he would have liked to possess, say, twenty thousand a year to bestow freely as he pleased. But as he had nothing in the world but a large number of unpaid debts, the case was different. He dreaded poverty only less than he dreaded death, and, like many others, he had to struggle for existence; and as existence for him involved the possession of a certain amount of worldly comforts, which he had no legitimate means of obtaining, he found himself under the necessity of making the wants of others subservient to his own, upon the accepted principle that necessity knows no law.

Picking his way back to the ford, with memory echoing the passionate message of Denise to Harry, he thought of the joy he could bring into those two lives by delivering it to him with a simple confession of the truth, and he asked himself if he could afford it. A very slight amount of consideration showed him that he could not afford it. What would he gain by clearing away the delusions that separated the husband and wife now, and promised to widen into an impassable gulf? Nothing—not a *maravedi!*

They would not be even commonly grateful
to him. Ignoring his self-sacrifice — attri-
buting it probably to fear, self-seeking, or
some baser motive — they would consider
only the sacrifice he had meditated making
of their happiness, and with no feeling (save
one of indignation), they would possibly turn
their backs on him, shut their door in his
face, and leave him to fare as he might, un-
assisted. No ; he certainly could not afford
it ; such self-sacrifice was not to be thought
of ; circumstances compelled him to profit
by the providential coincidences which had
already put him in possession of a well-stuffed
note-book.

Liz had given him the key of the back-
door that he might let himself in at will, she
having bolted the front-door as a protection
against the possible return of Thrale and
Lady Harding ; so he entered the cottage
noiselessly, and, finding the lower room

empty, stepped lightly upstairs, guessing that Liz was with Harding, and curious to know how they got on in his absence.

He found Liz seated on a low chair by the bedside, her fingers knotted upon her knees, her body bending forward, and her eyes fixed upon Harding's face with all the melting tenderness of a young mother. The General, in his quality of dilettante, stopped a moment to admire the pretty picture, thinking what a lot an artist chappie might make of the subject, if he could only render that look.

The door creaked on its old hinges as he pushed it wide to pass in. Liz started, raising her finger in alarm, for Harding slept; and a little murmur of regret came from her parted lips as Harding turned upon his pillow. His dream must have been sweet, his awaking even sweeter, for a smile played upon his lips, and he held forth his hand, saying softly :

' *You*, dear ?'

Liz quietly took his raised hand in hers, and held it close and tenderly. But as he opened his drowsy eyes and saw whose face it was that leaned towards him, the smile faded away, leaving only perplexity in its place, and, as his wandering glance fell upon the General, he drew his hand from Liz's, and closed his eyes again with a bitter sigh.

' It's only your friend, sir,' said Liz soothingly. ' *She* shan't come near you ; all the doors is bolted.'

Few and low as the words were that Denise had spoken the night before, the sound of her voice had reached Harding's ear, and he had questioned Liz, and heard her account of the interview, given with her belief that Denise and Thrale, companions in vice, and heartlessly self-seeking, had come with the hope of finding him a dead

man, and gone discomfited away, finding that
he lived.

Once more the General, looking down on
the boyish face, on which Old Care was mark-
ing the first lines in the contracted brow and
down-drawn lips, asked himself if he could
anyhow afford to realize his young friend's
dream of joy, and gave up the endeavour
as a useless job.

'If they want to see me die, let them
come!' Harding exclaimed suddenly, and in
passionate despair.

'There, there! don't you worry about them
—they're not worth it, dear boy,' said the
General. 'They'll bother us no more now.
I've just been into the village, and I find
they went away this morning.'

'This morning!'

'Yes; they stayed at the Wheatsheaf last
night.'

'Oh, think of that!' cried Liz indignantly,

ignoring the fact that it was impossible for them to leave the night before.

'And I might have been dying the while,' said Harding. 'It seems almost impossible, doesn't it? Those two who seemed so true and loyal to me!'

'About as bad as they make 'em,' remarked the General, in an off-handed tone of contempt, as he held out his arm, with a look to Liz to pull his sleeve. 'But that's the better reason for regarding their loss with indifference, isn't it, old chappie? A misdeal's only vexatious when you happen to hold the best cards in your hand. Good riddance to sad rubbish,' he continued, disengaging himself from his coat, and crossing to poke the fire. 'Shuffle up the damned cards, and begin all over again, with a better chance of good luck in the next deal. I remember when we were playing pool at Lord Newington's——' And he began to reel off with spirit one of his interminable yarns.

He was a capital story-teller, having an excellent memory, a large inventive faculty, some wit, and the tact to divergate into any channel that he perceived was agreeable to his audience. He could go on for hours when it suited him, and never weary, when, as in the present case, he saw his own advantage in making his chatter agreeable. To his ability as a ready *raconteur* he owed in a great measure his wide popularity, and the indulgence that most men extended, despite that shadowy something which clung to him.

He leant against the mantel-shelf, with his back to the fire and a cigar in the corner of his mouth, talking on and on, forcing Harding to listen, despite his disposition to brood over his grief, and, finally, to take interest, and find a feeble sort of amusement in the rambling narrative. It was all jargon and a pack of nonsense to Liz, the General having no interest in amusing her, and soon she slipped out of the room with a sigh, to think that she had not the old man's power to charm away Harding's bitter grief and distract his thoughts from his wrongs.

'By the way,' said he, in one of his many discursions, 'which route did you take when you went down South?'

'Through Belgium and Switzerland.'

'Beastly lot of changing. I always go along the Riviera, and generally stay there. Better climate than Naples, and much more lively. There's a snug little villa at Mentone that I can get for a mere song—close by the rail, and about ten minutes' run from Monte Carlo. Suit us to a T. Thinking of it just now as I waded through the slush. What a change! Cloudless sky, gardens one mass of roses, orange-grove one side, bit of an olive-wood on the other; mountains at the back shutting out the north and east winds, glorious sea in front, and Monte Carlo just round the point of Cap St. Martin. Take the grand express—shut your eyes upon all the misery on earth, and open them upon all the joys in creation.'

'It must be good,' said Harding, staring up at the beams. 'I shall be glad to get out of this—this awful place.'

'We'll be there in a fortnight, dear chappie, if Yardley's as good as his word,' cried the General gleefully.

Liz heard that through the door, and a feeling of hatred possessed her. Envy and jealousy rankled in her heart, and to such a degree that the General, on coming down to the chop he had ordered for his lunch, observed that something was wrong, by her pinched nostrils, her closed lips, and her averted glance, as much as by her lack of attention to his personal comforts.

' Been listening at the door again,' he said to himself. ' Taken a sudden dislike to me. This won't do. A single word from her may upset all my calculations. Must find out what's amiss and smooth her down.'

And therewith the wily tactician set himself to overcome Liz's silence, and make himself agreeable to *her*.

CHAPTER XVII.

ONLY A SLAVEY.

'How's your mamma this morning?' the General began.

'About the same, thank you,' replied Liz, whisking a clean napkin out of the dresser drawer.

'Has she had medical advice?'

'The doctor can't do nothing, he says.'

'That's a bad look-out for her—and you, too.'

Liz tossed her head to signify that it was useless to discuss that point, and, having spread her napkin on a tray, took the basin that was to contain Harding's beef-tea to the light to make sure it was speckless ; and the General, slowly munching a piece of bread, leant back in his chair and admired the pleasant outline of her figure in silhouette, her pretty profile, the light playing upon a straying curl in the nape of her neck.

'I should like to see you in a cap, Liz,' he observed.

'Why ?' she asked, turning upon him sharply.

'It would become you well—set off your pretty hair to advantage.'

Liz had in her time received so many compliments, from young as well as elderly gentlemen, that she cared little for this one.

'Oh, I thought you fancied the gentleman might like me better in a cap.'

'Perhaps he would.'

She set down the basin, took something from another drawer, went into the scullery, and presently reappeared in a dainty little muslin cap with long strings.

'Very fetching,' observed the General.

Liz had not asked for his opinion, and, taking no notice of it, poured the beef-tea from the saucepan into the basin.

'There's no prettier costume in the world than the English domestic servant's of to-day.'

Liz cut the dry toast in fingers, contemptuously silent. She wasn't in service now, and wouldn't have put on this badge of servitude to please anyone—except the gentleman upstairs, who might feel freer to accept her attentions if he knew she was only a servant.

'There's only one costume that comes any way near it for smartness,' continued the General in the same equal tones.

Liz would have given anything to know what that costume was; but she would not ask him, when all he thought about was getting the gentleman away as soon as he could to some foreign part, where she should never, never go. So she carried the tray upstairs, still wondering about that costume, and the General finished his chop alone.

She stayed with Harding till he had drunk his tea, shaking up and smoothing his pillow, busying herself about the room, and talking chiefly about the weather. He smiled gratefully at her when she drew the bedclothes tenderly over his shoulders, and she came down in better temper, apologizing to the General for being so long, and hastening to remove his plate, and set the cheese and butter before him.

'Did he admire your cap?' asked the General.

'I think so. He looked very kind at me. But he didn't say much, being so weak and down-hearted, poor gentleman!'

'It will do him good to see you now and

then. He's been used to women's society, and would feel the loss of it if you weren't here to look after him. I can distract his thoughts—that's good in its way ; but you can soothe him, and that's better.'

Liz was delighted, but she said nothing to that effect, only she asked the General if he wouldn't have a glass of ale with his cheese instead of that sour stuff, indicating the Beaune sent down from the Wheatsheaf by the General's order. The General declined the mixture.

' What costume was that you were talking about ?' Liz asked presently. She was quite ' friends ' with the General now, and if only he would not take the gentleman away so soon, he would have been really nice in her estimation.

' A nurse's.'

' A nurse? Oh, I don't think much of that !' she said, with disapprobation in her voice.

' I don't mean the ordinary black and white affair, but something artistic—something that a lady might wish to wear—a nice soft material that falls in pretty folds.'

' Cashmere ?'

' Yes ; that would do—cashmere of a pale slatey-blue.'

' Silver-gray.'

' With a nice lining to harmonize.'

' Red ?'

' 'M no ; I should say blue.'

' Blue would look very nice when the cape fell back.'

' The usual white cuffs and collars, and then a dear little Dutch bonnet with a narrow white frill '—the General looked at the girl with the half-closed eyes of an æsthetic critic —' with a sort of a scoop at the back to allow your hair being seen in loose curls.'

' Rolls ?'

' Or a bun, if they keep in fashion.'

'Misseses won't let you wear 'em,' said Liz with a sigh.

'Do you hanker very greatly after going into service again?'

'Not me! I'm sick and tired of it. But once a servant, always a servant, they say, if a girl wants to keep straight. It ain't no good me thinking of being a hospital nurse; I'm too old, for one thing, to begin, and I couldn't afford to go in for all the probationing and things.'

'Still, a clever, pleasant, nice-looking girl might be a nurse to an invalid without the requirements of a hospital nurse.'

Liz, crossing the room, stopped suddenly, and turned, breathless, to know by the General's look if he 'meant anything' by these hints. The General ignored her questioning regard, and, filling his glass, asked if she had written to her sisters.

'Not yet. Why?'

'I was only thinking that this must be a terribly dull life for a lively girl like you.'

'Oh, I can't stand it! I love mother better than they do; but to stay here and see no one from week's end to week's end, it's enough to make one wicked.'

'That's what I thought. But if your sisters refuse to help you——'

'Oh, I don't know what I shall do—indeed I don't!' The girl's eyes filled with tears in anticipation of approaching solitude.

'I suppose someone in the village would take care of the old lady for a trifle?'

'Why, there's Aunt Fanny at Whetstone, she'd take her for five shillings a week and be glad; but we can't afford that—and me out of work.'

'But if you found employment—remunerative employment?'

Liz couldn't speak; the long words or the suspense of hope and fear seemed to choke her.

'Say a pound a week.'

'A pound a week?' Liz gasped.

'With a complete outfit, including that becoming costume we have been talking about.'

'What do you mean?' she asked, coming to the table, and setting her hands upon it as she made the demand. 'You ain't making a fool of me, are you?'

'I wish your hands were a little whiter, and your nails——'

'Oh, my hands are white enough when I ain't got to mess about in cold water, and I can keep my nails as good as a lady's when there ain't any fires to make.'

'You wouldn't have to mess about in water or make fires if you could direct servants to do such work for you.'

'For Heaven's sake, sir, do tell me what you mean. You are driving me nearly crazy with these hints.'

'This is what I mean, Miss Hardacre,'

said the General, pushing aside his plate, laying his arms upon the table, and bending towards Liz with the most serious expression on his face : 'When we get to the South, I must have some gentle, pleasant young woman to act as a kind of nurse and companion to Sir Henry Harding—one who can see that his domestic comforts '—he might have added 'and mine,' but he did not—'are properly attended to—someone who can stroll amongst the flowers, sit by his side, or, in my absence '—'at Monte Carlo' was also unsaid—'could read to him——'

'I ain't a scholard !'

'Or chat to him about trifles, which would be better,' said the General, repairing his oversight. 'Gossip about the people who pass, the little incidents that occur ; take him out for drives in a carriage ; find out what is going on at the theatre or the casino, and induce him to go there.'

'Oh, do you think I could do that?'

'I am sure you could—if you would.'

'If I would. Why, I'd give everything I've got in the world for such a life.'

'Well, we can think it over.'

'Why, it don't want any thinking about.'

'Nevertheless, a few days' consideration will do no harm.'   The General foresaw that his chops would be more carefully cooked for such consideration. 'If we make up our minds by the end of the week, there will still be ample time to dispose of your mamma and get your costume made. We must certainly have that costume, and for this reason: it will prevent any misconstruction being set upon your relations to Sir Henry and myself. For it is the most natural thing that an invalid should be attended by a nurse, and so your future prospects will not be endangered by this arrangement.'

Mightily the General cared for the future

prospects of this poor girl, or the consequences to her happiness of this association
with Harding! If Denise could be sacrificed
to ensure his possession of life's pleasures,
what weight would the welfare of a mere
servant-girl have in his consideration? Of
what earthly good are women if they cannot
be turned to the use of man? The best in
the land are not too good for his purpose;
but a girl of the ordinary servant-girl class—
well, as Liz clearly showed, that kind of
person should feel only too happy if she
could be employed to this end.

CHAPTER XVIII.

THE BEGINNING OF MARTYRDOM.

WITH that determination to 'be good and patient,' Denise returned to the Court, buoyant with hope now that she was unburdened of crushing suspicion, eager to seek the happiest aspect of the situation and find good in everything.

Thrale's guarded acceptance of her views, his reticence and obvious constraint, and his irresponsiveness, chafed her.

'You are not half glad enough,' she said, with vexation. 'You make me feel, Bernard, as if I should like to shake you.'

'Perhaps it's because I have been so

much shaken that I am so dull,' he replied evasively.

In truth, with his foresight of future probabilities, he had little reason to be gay. The General had not attempted to deceive him as to the nature of this expedient for reconciling Denise. It was nothing but a subterfuge—a mere house of cards that must be overthrown by the first breath of truth, and he hated himself for being party to the lie. To his straightforward mind it would have been better to let Denise know the worst, for which the first shock had prepared her, than to foster hopes which must surely be destroyed later on. This seemed to him as cruel a kindness as resuscitating a dead heart only to make it suffer again the pangs of death.

He lunched with Denise, miserably ill at ease, incapable of playing the hypocrite well or of following his honest instincts.

'You are not afraid of—of anything?' Denise asked timidly, after a long pause, in which she had vainly been seeking to account for Bernard being so unlike himself.

'Afraid?' he replied, in a guarded tone of interrogation.

'Afraid that the doctor misunderstands dear Harry's condition?'

'Oh no; he seems to thoroughly comprehend the nature of his accident. I heard him explaining it to the General last night in almost the same terms that Dr. Arbuthnot used in describing his first accident five years ago. And the treatment he prescribes is exactly the same — absolute isolation and repose.'

'I will not go to him until the doctor sends to say I may.'

'That is advisable, however strange and hard it may seem to you.'

'It should not be either, if I have faith in

the doctor, and surely he must be wiser than I,' responded Denise, employing the argument by which she had succeeded partially in taking a 'reasonable' view of the case, and overcoming her womanly revolt against the enforced separation from her husband in his sickness. 'And two or three weeks is not long to wait,' she continued; 'it will all be forgotten when he comes back to me.'

She murmured a little coo of joy in anticipation of that happiness, when she should have her dear husband once more, and all to herself, to care for and to nurse, as she felt none other could. And then, turning to Thrale with a yearning for sympathy, she was more vexed than ever by his silence and the gloom on his face as he bent over his plate.

' I wish he would go away,' she said in her anger to herself. ' I would ten times rather be alone. How can one be hopeful and cheerful with such a dreadful wet-blanket upon one ? When Harry comes home and finds him here, he will think I wanted him to stay—like a silly girl who is afraid to be left alone.'

It was a positive relief to her when Thrale, looking at his watch, asked if he might order a trap to take him over to the station. She rang the bell at once to give the order.

'Are you going to Ridingford?' she asked.

'No; to London.'

She was glad to hear that—jealously glad —for if she might not see her husband and watch over him, surely his friend should not. Her feeling of irritation withheld her from asking any questions about his movements, as he offered no explanation ; and she said good-bye quite coldly in parting.

But the trap had scarcely started before the revulsion of feeling came, and her heart was wrung by the consciousness of her ingratitude to this friend, who had alone stood by her and shared her misery of the preceding day. Why, it struck her now for the first time, he was to have sailed yesterday for India—his passage had been taken a week ago—and without a word, as if it were a matter of course, he had abandoned his purpose for her sake. And now it flashed upon her, with the shock of a sudden awaking, that, finding he was no longer needed, he had taken up his purpose again as quickly as he had dropped it, and was even now on his way to the East—dismissed without one gentle word of gratitude or farewell, never, perhaps, to return—he who, next to her husband, was the dearest friend she had. His depression and silence, which had so unreasonably vexed her, were explained at once. Oh, what a selfish, mean little fool she had been to lose sight of everything but her own happiness! She started to the door with the hope that he might not be beyond recall—that she might yet beckon him back to acknowledge her faults and beg him to forgive her. But the trap was now far up the avenue, and Thrale, bending his head to meet the cruel wind, did not look back.

The tears of remorse rushed into her eyes, and she furtively drew out her handkerchief to stanch them before re-entering the house. A suppressed titter at her back quickened her jaded spirit like the cut of a whip, and turning sharply, with indignation tingling in every vein, she caught sight of a cluster of servants vanishing out of sight into the service passage ; only one, more impudent than the rest, stood her ground, and, having treated her to an insolent stare, turned with a toss of her head and followed the rest with the haughty carriage of an upper servant.

What was the meaning of this insult ? Denise asked herself as she entered the drawing-room. How dared these women, her servants, watch her actions and make sport of her unhappiness? What excuse could Evans offer for her effrontery and the contemptuous regard with which she audaciously turned her back upon her mistress? Smarting under the indignity offered her, Denise rang the bell, resolved to have these questions answered at once.

'Tell Evans to come to me,' she said, when Mrs. Austin, the housekeper, appeared.

'Certainly, my lady, if you wish it; but,' closing the door and dropping her voice, 'if I might make so bold, I would advise you not. Evans gave warning this morning, and she would like nothing better than to openly insult you before all; and she might say such shocking things, my lady, being very smart-tongued, that I really don't think you could expect any respectable servant to stay. Jennings and Jane Smith has already given their month's notice.'

'You will pay them their wages and send them away this afternoon.'

'Certainly, my lady ; and I'm very sorry, but if you could suit yourself with another housekeeper—you see, my lady, when accidents of this kind happen in a family, our reputation is likely to suffer if——'

'Bring me your accounts, and—and leave the room immediately,' said Denise, choking with humiliation and anger.

For a day and a half they had talked of nothing in the servants' hall but of Harding's mad flight, and the subsequent behaviour of Denise and Thrale. From the butler to the page, the lady's-maid to the scullery-wench, everyone had been gleaning evidence to add to the common store of misconception and wilful misrepresentation, taking example and profiting by the malevolence, maybe, of those who had not ill-breeding for their excuse. Starting with the presumption that Thrale and Denise were guilty, it is easy to imagine the construction put upon their absence at night, their return together, and the tears of Denise when Bernard drove away. Weak in judgment, strong in prejudice, they in a moment stripped their mistress of every pure and gentle attribute she possessed, and clothed her in the most villainous tissue of infamy their mischievous ingenuity could patch together from the scraps of slander that came in their way.

If Denise had been guilty, if she had harboured only one disloyal thought even, she might have perceived that suspicion lay upon her ; but, being innocent, that was quite impossible, and she could only conclude that rumours circulated in Rockingham of her husband's liaison with Liz Hardacre, and that the idle servants had magnified and distorted the circumstances attending his accident into some horrible proof of infidelity. That was quite possible ; for had not she herself been misled by those circumstances with the wickedest doubts — doubts which even now, despite herself, were not wholly banished from her heart ?   It was not for her to undeceive those servants or anyone else who chose to think ill of her husband, for that would have given countenance to suspicion ; but she prayed that he might come quickly back, to prove to all the world that he was her loyal and true Harry.

As soon as Thrale had pulled off his gloves, he wrote to Denise from his hotel in London :

'MY DEAR LADY HARDING,

'I find I can postpone my departure for a month without inconvenience.   This gives me the hopeful prospect of our meeting again at the Court under the happiest of conditions before I leave England. You will, of course, hear from Harry, and you may imagine what pleasure it will give me to hear good tidings through you.

'Ever faithfully yours,

'BERNARD THRALE.'

By return he received a reply from Denise that pained him inexpressibly, such sorrow and humility were betrayed by the touching phrases of regret and gratitude. He seemed to see the writer's tears; and at a certain point he felt she must have paused to brush them away, and set herself to resume with gentle courage.

But that she should already have to struggle for strength to write cheerfully told its tale.

'Her martyrdom has begun,' he said to himself. 'Where will it end?'

Reason forbade him to go to her—bade

him wait on for the inevitable development which would permit him to leave Denise for ever, or make him more necessary to her than ever he had yet been.

'If I am wanted, I shall know only too soon,' he said to himself.

And one day, when he opened a telegram, the following words came to him as a foregone conclusion :

' I am in great trouble.   Please come.

'DENISE.'

CHAPTER XIX.

THE GENERAL SCORES ANOTHER TRICK.

LOOKING from the window as the train ran into the station at Rockingham, Thrale descried Denise standing on the platform a little apart from the waiting passengers. He had telegraphed by what train he was coming, and was not surprised to see her; but without that preparation he almost doubted if he should have recognised her, so haggard and ill she looked, so much older for the mental strain of these two past weeks.

'He is gone!' she said, with distraction in her voice and in her regard as he took her hand. 'Gone away,' she added, as if to convey to him more clearly the thing which she herself could scarcely realize.

He passed her hand through his arm and led her up the platform away from the crowd, for her emotion was too violent for restraint, and the tears were now running fast down her wan cheeks.

The Vicar and his wife, old friends, were coming down the platform ; they were too close to be avoided, and as they passed Thrale raised his hat. The Vicar kept his eyes fixed well before him, but his wife, in a less Christian spirit, looked Thrale straight in the face, with a drawn upper lip and stony regard, without making the slightest response to his salutation. In astonishment Thrale glanced at Denise ; her chin was upon her breast.

'Lift up your head, dear friend ; *you* have done no wrong,' he said.

She shook her head, but could not answer him, or trust herself to speak until they had come to the end of the platform. Then, stifling her agitation, and with forced calm, she said, in broken sentences :

'I knew you would come, and yet—I did not know. Everyone is against me—and there is nothing to hope for. Must I go back to the Court ?'

'Unless you feel the need of a woman's sympathy. We men are most helpless things, you know. We seldom know the right thing to do or say, and seldomer how to do or say it. How would it be if we went to Mrs. Balfour ? We know she is a good, kind soul.'

'Is she, do you think ?'

'The best that I know.'

She stopped, and, looking into his face, said :

'Then how bad I must be, Bernard : for she will not see me—will not let me speak to her !'

'Why, what have you done ?'

' I do not know.'

' Surely there is some mistake in this. Perhaps she was not at home.'

' No one is at home to me. When not a friend called or sent to know if Harry was alive or dead, I felt I must call on them, to show that Harry had done me no wrong, as I thought. But everyone denied me. And then, when this news came, I went again to Mrs. Balfour, and sent in a note I had written, telling her I was in great trouble, and wished to speak to her.' The words choked her as she spoke.

' And then——' said Thrale gently.

' And then she sent back my note with a cruel message, saying that she did not wish to see me.'

Thrale led her out of the station in the greatest perplexity. The brougham stood there ; he opened the door with a significant gesture, and, when she was seated, he told the coachman to drive home, and took his place by her side.

'Where is the General?' he asked, when they were on their way to the Court, his thoughts in the midst of this mystery turning to Gordon by some process of natural selection.

'He came over on Monday. He has been several times. First he came to pay the servants who wished to go. For when I dismissed the housekeeper, I found to my humiliation that I had no money to pay her. You don't know how they have made me suffer. It was dreadful. They made me feel that *I* was the guilty one. I could not bear it. It seemed such an insult to him— whom I thought was quite good and true to me. All the maid-servants are gone, Bernard ; I should have been without any-one in the house if the gardener's wife had not come in.'

' But the General,' said Thrale with tender firmness, hoping to distract her thoughts from these past tortures, and to get to the bottom of the mystery.

' He came on Monday evening, and, finding me very low-spirited, he stayed till the next morning—yesterday. And he made me so happy ! I hardly knew myself when I went up to dress for dinner—I looked quite young again. He told me that Harry was almost well, and that the doctor consented to his coming home, and he asked me if I would go back with him to fetch Harry. And it was as much as I could do to refuse ; but I did, thinking it would be better for him, and that he would feel less constraint about— about that woman.'

' What did the General say about her ?'

' He said she had become very reasonable and good, and consented to some proposal he had made to set her up in a little business.'

'Did he tell you why she was to be pro-
vided for in that way ?'

'No ; but it would have been only right
to repay her for—for——' She hesitated a
moment, and then, breaking through her
reserve, she said impulsively : 'Oh, Bernard,
I knew it ! I felt that there must be something more than was told me ; but I—I
conquered myself, and made up my mind
that it should make no difference in my love
for Harry—that I would never reproach him,
or say a word that should hurt him or remind
him of the past.'

Oh, what nights of struggle, and self-sup-
pression, and bending of the knee in sub-
mission to cruel injustice, and agony of death
and new birth, must have been spent to
attain to such resignation, thought Thrale.

'And,' he said, taking Denise's hand in
his and pressing it, with the love of a brother
in his heart, 'to take one trouble singly at

a time—and then yesterday morning the General went back to Ridingford.'

'Yes; promising he would bring Harry back in the afternoon. And we made the house as bright as if all our servants were about—I and Mrs. Bates; and I cooked the dinner myself—the things Harry used to like best. And we sat up till midnight, and even then I could not give up hoping, but listened to every sound, and jumped up once with my heart beating awfully, thinking I heard wheels in the avenue—but it was only the wind in the laurels.'

'And this morning, dear friend?' interposed Thrale.

'This morning a letter came—this,' said she, drawing a limp and creased sheet from her muff, and putting it in Thrale's hand.

He opened it, and, leaning to the window, found light enough to read the General's

fine, bold hand.   The letter was dated from
the Cosmopolitan Hotel, London.

'DEAR LADY HARDING' (the old rascal
wrote, clearly foreseeing that it would be read
by others),

'I hardly know how to break the appalling
news which I may no longer withhold from
you ; and I can only pray Heaven to give you
the fortitude to bear with resignation this last
and least expected blow.

'To my consternation, when I arrived at
the cottage at the ford this morning, I found
every door and window securely fastened,
and no sign of any living inmate.   They
were gone, your faithless husband and the
abandoned and crafty woman who has so
completely deceived me by hypocritical pro-
fessions of repentance and pretended willing-
ness to sever her connection with Sir Henry
Harding for a pecuniary consideration.   As

the truth dawned upon me, and my thoughts turned to you, I could only thank Heaven that you had declined to act upon my suggestion ; for had you been with me at the moment, you must have suffered again all the agony you endured a fortnight since, without the consolation of hope which I was then enabled to offer, and I know not what we should have done !'

'There's truth in that admission, at any rate,' thought Thrale. 'The selfish old rascal was more affected by the consideration of his own possible embarrassment and inconvenience than by this poor woman's agony.'

'Fearing the worst, I repaired to Dr. Yardley—who will, I am sure, give you further particulars if you wish for them—and learnt from him that half an hour after

I had left Ridingford to run over to you,
Miss Hardacre ordered a couple of carriages
to be sent down from the Wheatsheaf ; in
one her bedridden mother was sent to a
relative living in a neighbouring village ; in
the other she and Sir Harry Harding were
taken to the railway-station. At Ridingford
Station there was no lack of information.
The porters had helped an invalid gentleman
out of the fly, and found a first-class compartment in the up-train for him and the
young woman ; the booking-clerk said that
she had taken tickets for London. What
was I to do, my dear Lady Harding ? Should
I return to you with these hopeless tidings,
or should I pursue the fugitives with a view
to making one last appeal to Harding's sense
of honour, and retrieving him if possible from
the ruin that surely awaits him ? Reason
bade me take the latter course, and accord-
ingly I came up to London by the very next

train.   Here, however, all trace of these misguided runaways was lost, and, despite most searching inquiries, I have failed to obtain any clue to their movements.   But rest assured, dear Lady Harding, that I shall not relax my exertions or abandon this pursuit until I have run Harding to earth, and compelled him, if not to return to you, at least to make such substantial repara-tion——'

Thrale stopped there.

' You do not wish to see this again ?' he asked, turning to Denise.

' Oh, no, no !' she answered.

He crushed it up and thrust it in his pocket, less disgusted by the old man's selfishness and shallow pretexts for escaping any responsibility he might have as the nearest friend of Lady Harding's father—for these were scarcely more than he should have

expected from the plausible old humbug—
than astonished by the flagrant indelicacy of
one who passed in society as a gentleman,
suggesting at such a time as this a pecuniary
indemnity to the stricken wife for such misery
as Harding had inflicted.

Yet he perceived that the question of a
material arrangement must be met before long,
and he was not sorry to read the letter Denise
found awaiting her when they arrived at the
Court. It was from Fielder and Playfair,
solicitors, of Lincoln's Inn, and ran thus :

' MADAM,

'We are instructed by Sir Henry
Harding to consult you immediately with
regard to a settlement of your claims upon
his estate. If you will kindly let us know the
earliest date at which it may suit your con-
venience to see us, we shall wait upon you
with the utmost promptitude.'

With Lady Harding's consent, Thrale despatched a telegram at once, saying that she would be at home the following afternoon to receive the solicitors.

CHAPTER XX.

AN APPEAL.

Soon after lunch the next day a fly from Rockingham brought Mr. Playfair and his clerk to the Court, and without delay they were introduced to the library, where Denise and Thrale were awaiting the interview. Denise, despite the fluttering of her heart between a dread consciousness that her fate was now to be sealed, and the ever lingering hope of unexpected reprieve, received the lawyer with unassuming dignity, that was not lost upon the shrewd, observant little man. Oh, if Harry could be redeemed —it had come to that—no one in the world should ever know of his disgrace through her.

Having discussed the customary generalities with much suavity, while his clerk, taking a seat at the further end of the table, whipped out a stylograph and a quire of foolscap, Mr. Playfair, facing his chair more directly to Denise, said, smoothing one hand gently over the other, and speaking with slow and very distinct articulation :

'To come to a matter of more serious nature, Lady Harding, permit me to say at the outset I am entirely ignorant of the causes leading to the arrangement we are about to make.   Our client, Sir Henry Harding, wished us to understand that those causes, so far as we are concerned, are entirely irrelevant to the transaction with which we are entrusted.'

'He hadn't even the common decency to exonerate her,' thought Thrale, looking at

Denise ; but he held his tongue, divining by the look in the poor wife's face that she would rather suffer by unjust suspicion than have this stranger know of her husband's frailty.

'That transaction,' continued Mr. Playfair, 'is of a purely financial character, and the object in view is to arrive at an amicable, and at the same time legal, understanding upon the question of maintenance. To come at once to the point, madam, we are empowered to meet your demands within any reasonable limit.'

The little lawyer drew himself up and beamed upon Denise, happy to offer so charming a lady such admirable terms.

'*I* make no demand,' said she quietly. 'I ask my husband for nothing.' And then, as Mr. Playfair raised his eyebrows and fixed his eyes upon his joined thumbs in perplexity at this unexpected contingency, she added in the same even tone, 'What does he ask of me?'

'Sir Henry makes no stipulation or condition whatever, and I can think of only one decision on his part which can give rise to any objection on yours.'

'What is that?'

'I refer to the decision which involves your change of residence.'

'Do you mean that I am to leave this house—my home?' she asked quickly, her pale cheek flushing with the cruel suspicion that Harry intended to bring that woman here to take her place.

'That, I fear, madam, is a matter of necessity.'

'And what if I decline to go, decline to be turned out like a dishonest servant?' she asked with rising indignation, as that jealous fear rankled in her breast.

'In that case we must apply for further

instructions. Although,' added Mr. Playfair reflectively, ' if you cling greatly to residing here, it might be possible for you to make terms with the purchaser of the estate——'

' Sir Henry proposes to sell up,' Thrale suggested as a clearer explanation.

' Everything ; except, of course, such personal effects as you may claim, Lady Harding.'

Denise looked round her with dismay, her eyes resting on the rows of books in their beautiful binding of ivory vellum, heirlooms of the family that Harry prized so dearly ; on many a rare and costly object they had bought together in their honeymoon, in Florence and Rome and elsewhere, to adorn their home—things that they had admired again and again standing in this old room, hand-in-hand, lovers still. There was no jealousy in her heart now—only dismay and the anguish of irrecoverable loss. Was the disaster so irretrievable that he could never return ?   Had he given up everything, abandoned all, in the consciousness that nothing could ever induce him to live again in the old home ?

' Oh, where is he ?' she cried, springing to her feet as if to fly to him.

' I regret, madam, that I cannot possibly answer your question.'

' I must see him—indeed I must,' she entreated.

' I can only repeat, with great pain, that I am powerless to help you.'

' Oh, Bernard, this must not be !' she cried. ' We must not let him carry out this hasty project.   Think how proud he is of the old house and all the dear things in it, all that he has inherited from generations and genera- tions—he, the last of all the family ; think how bitterly he will regret this when—when —when he is better and strong again.

Think, sir,' she added, turning to the little
lawyer with humble pleading in her voice,
her melting eyes, her outstretched quivering
hands, and the very carriage of her body—
'think, sir, my husband and I have never
had a bitter word—no, not one unkind word
or one ungentle glance since we were married.
And that is only a few months. We were
married in June. It isn't possible that he
can give up all he loves and prizes for
ever, and go away never to come back. He
has had an accident, and there has been a
little trouble since. Nothing so great that
we should live ever more strangers to each
other—nothing that may not be forgotten
soon.'

The lawyer shook his head despondingly
—a few guineas for this journey and that
speedy conclusion of the transaction were not
what he looked forward to.

'Tell him, sir,' continued Denise, 'tell him

that you found me very reasonable—that I am not so foolish a woman as he thinks, and that I may grow wiser still as I get older. Tell him I agree to everything except this— and this chiefly for his sake. Ask him to stay only a little while before he sells his old home, and the beautiful trees, and all the things he was fond of. A few months will make no difference. And see, I will give him a proof how reasonable I can be. I will go away from here to-morrow, and never come back till he bids me come. I will leave everything—mine as well as his. I will take nothing at all, to show how certain I am that he will come again and send for me.'

'Perhaps, madam,' suggested Mr. Playfair, 'if you wrote this touching appeal in a letter——'

'Why, so I will. I never thought of that. I will go to my room and write it now, and you will take it.'

'With the greatest pleasure.'

'And you will take no action until you have his answer?'

'Certainly not.'

'Oh, thank you. I will not be very long.'

And the poor little soul hurried from the room, convinced that at last she had hit upon the reasonable thing to do.

'It can be only an infatuation,' she said to herself, as she ran upstairs; 'and if his love for me was no more than that, why, then he may outlive this second as he outlived the first. Nay, he must wish for me a little. Our hearts have beat together. He can't forget me altogether.'

As she sat down to write her letter, Thrale took a sheet of paper and delivered himself of his feelings:

'For God's sake be a man, Harry, and not a contemptible cad. Think of this dear little wife of yours overcoming every feeling of resentment and jealousy, hiding her own griefs and your fault to keep an opening for your escape from this dishonourable situation. Think not of the few weeks of unhallowed pleasure before you, but of the years of bitter repentance that must follow, of the degradation and humiliation to which you are willingly subjecting yourself. Think how truly and tenderly this wife has loved you, how bravely for your sake she is now suffering martyrdom, and think of the ruin you bring upon a gentle soul whose only fault is that she loved you too confidingly. Think how the woman suffers in the position you impose upon her; how pitiless the judgment of society is upon the woman parted from her husband, how unjust the sentence, and how terrible the penalty exacted. Rouse yourself, get out of this horrible mess by one vigorous effort—if not for the sake of poor

Denise, for your own. I say nothing of
myself save that I hope to grasp your hand
as I've grasped it before when you've done
the right and plucky thing, and say again,
" Well done, Harry !"

'BERNARD.'

The two letters were duly forwarded to
Harding, Hôtel Meurice, Paris. He, utterly
careless whether letters came or not—only
praying that he might not be troubled by
any reference to that which he wished buried
in forgetfulness—very willingly relegated to
the General all correspondence that was
necessary with his lawyers ; and the General,
still alert to the ticklish tenure of his pros-
perity, kept a sharp eye on the postman, and
when Mr. Playfair's letter came, enclosing
those from Denise and Thrale, and asking
for instructions, the General read all, dropped
two in the fire, and poked them well between

the blazing logs, and simply replied to the lawyer that Sir Henry Harding saw no reason for altering his decision or replying to the letters enclosed, and that he desired Harding Court to be put up for immediate sale without any further delay.

CHAPTER XXI.

ONLY A LITTLE CAST-OFF WIFE.

A WEEK elapsed before Denise heard from Harding's solicitors—a week of deferred hope for her, so exhausting in its effect that her overstrained and wearied spirit seemed to have lost its susceptibility to joy or pain. When the letter came, saying that 'Sir Henry Harding saw no reason to alter his decision, and desired his affairs to be wound up without further delay,' she read it almost apathetically.

'There is no hope now,' she said, putting the letter in Bernard's hand.

He had foreseen this for the past few days,

knowing that if Harry's heart and conscience were to be touched at all, his first impulse on reading his wife's letter would be to telegraph at once and end her suffering.

He laid the letter aside, but held the hand that gave it in his, as he said :

'We must think of him as one that is dead.'

'Oh, if he were I could still love him—I should cry to think of him, and ease my heart.   But see, my eyes are dry, my tears all dried up, and I feel that something has gone from me, here, here,' said she, pressing her breast—'something good and sweet that can never come there again.   It is love that is gone—love that used to make me feel that God was there and would never let me do a wrong thing to anyone on earth.'

Oh for a woman's tongue to soothe and console, the intuitive power to strike some sympathetic chord and fill this mute soul with tender harmony! Thrale could think of nothing but platitudes, wholly inadequate to express his feeling of pity and commiseration, which, indeed, were inexpressible.

'Every bereavement must leave us with that sense of void——'

'But not this sense of degradation,' she retorted quickly, 'not this feeling of cruel injustice that makes one's brain swim with a craving for revenge; with thoughts of murder and reckless wickedness. Oh!' she cried, springing to her feet and snatching her hand from his passionately, 'I am afraid of myself. You do not know how bad a woman I may be.'

'I know how good a woman you have been,' he said, rising and going to her side, 'and I know that no one can do wrong who has struggled so bravely to do right.'

He led her back to her seat, and she made no resistance, exhausted now that the paroxysm of passion was past, and he sat beside her, taking her hand again, saying what he could to tranquillize her.

'Love and hate, grief and joy, all have their seasons, and none lasts for ever. The fiercest storm is soonest over, and happily the darker days are fewer than the bright in our little year. These dull clouds look as if they would never lift, don't they? yet we know that before long they will break, and the sun will shine down and warm the whole world into flower and song again.'

In this strain he talked on for some time, quite careless whether the thing he said was sensible or not, only conscious that if it did her good it was worth the saying; and she would now and then look up into his face with wondering gratitude in her eyes and a fluttering sigh, moved not so much by what he said as by the feeling that she had yet one friend who cared for her.

'I don't know whether you're aware, my lady,' said the gardener's wife, entering the room after a discreet knock and a pause, 'but the gentleman as brought the letter is a-waiting for an answer.'

'I will bring it to him presently,' said Thrale, and, taking up the lawyer's letter, he glanced down the pages.

After signifying Harding's intentions, Mr. Playfair wrote :

'In accordance with our client's instructions, we shall proceed at once to put his estate upon the market. Our Mr. Watson, the bearer of this letter, is empowered to render your ladyship every assistance in the removal of such personal effects as you may wish to reserve, to discharge all outstanding obligations, and to close the house as early as it may be convenient to surrender possession.

'With regard to the question we had the honour to discuss with you on the 18th inst., we beg you will let us know with as little delay as possible your estimate of the amount which should be placed to your credit at our bankers', resting assured that we shall be pleased to meet any reasonable demand on your part.'

Dropping the letter on his knee, Thrale turned to Denise.

'I will go away to-day,' she said with feverish haste, anticipating the question on his lips, 'and I will take nothing that he has ever given me—nothing! I will go away as poor as I came. See, this is the dress I wore before I was married—this poor frock that he used to admire.'

She had worn none other for the past week, and this perhaps with some sentimental notion that when Harry came back it would recall the old time and revive the old love.

'You are quite sure——' Thrale said, rising.

'Quite, quite,' she answered passionately. 'He has treated me as if I were not his wife; but the shame of it shall be his, not mine.'

Thrale inclined his head and left the room. He ordered the brougham to be brought to the door, saw Mr. Watson, and then with thoughtful consideration sent the gardener's wife to fetch Lady Harding's hat and mantle from her bedroom. Returning to Denise, he found the poor woman near the door, her hand resting upon the wall for support.

'I am so weak, so weak,' she murmured faintly. 'Yet I am doing right, Bernard, am I not?'

'I would not have you undo anything,' he answered. 'Take my arm—so. Now we will walk up and down a bit; that will give us strength. It was certain to be a hard wrench at the last.'

'I—I couldn't find courage to go upstairs for my things.'

'That's all right ; Mrs. Denham has gone for them.'

'You seem to know just how I feel, and yet I am so contradictory to myself, wavering between one thing and the other. I know I must go. I know I could not stay here ; and yet it is all so unreal, so difficult to under-stand, that I am to forsake all the past and begin a new life.'

'It will be easier by-and-by. I have ordered the brougham.'

'There's poor Sandy barking. Does he know that his mistress is going to leave him, I wonder ?'

Mrs. Denham brought in her things, and at a sign from Thrale withdrew quickly. He put the mantle on her shoulders, and she pinned her hat and drew the gloves upon her trembling hands as best she could. Soon after that the carriage wheels scrunched in the frost-bound drive, and Denise, pressing her lips closely together and lifting her drooping head, rose and took Bernard's arm. Looking neither to the right nor left, but walking as if in a trance, she passed through the hall and crossed the threshold of her lost home. The collie in the yard howled piteously—as dogs are said to do at the approach of death; and Denise wished it might be the end of her own miserable life that was so heralded.

They had left the Court some distance behind them, when Denise broke the long spell of silence that had fallen upon them.

'Where am I going?' she asked in a wondering tone, which showed that the question had but just dawned upon her.

' I have told the man to drive us to Rockingham.   Whether you stay there or not
must depend on your feeling.'

' I have not thought of it.   There were so
many things to think of—greater than what
is to become of me.'

' To me that seems the greatest of all,' he
said gravely.

She laughed hysterically.

' Why, I am nothing—a little cast-off wife,
that's all.   Who cares what end I come
to ?'

' I do.'

His tone abashed her, and she hung her
head, conscious of her ingratitude to this
generous friend.

' Is it nothing to me whether you sink or
swim, whether you throw up your arms and
go down, or reach the firm earth by a brave
effort ?   I do not doubt which you will do—
nor you either, deep down in your heart.

You're not a coward, nor a useless little member of society.'

She passed her hand through his arm, and pressed it, to show that she was not really ungrateful; then, after ruminating silently on his words and taking a practical view of them, she said :

' I'm not sure that I *am* a useful person, Bernard. Of course I must earn my living somehow, now that I have nothing in the world. I must do that; I *couldn't* rely upon other people's charity—I mean kindness.'

Thrale nodded with a smile of encouragement, happy to find that he had struck the right chord this time.

' Besides, I should like to work, so perhaps, after all, I am a useful person at heart. I have done it before, you know. Why, when I was fourteen I kept mother. Only then it was different. I don't think I should like to go on the stage now, even if they would have me, and I scarcely believe they would, because I am getting so ugly and dull.   Still, there are other things a woman can do.   The worst of it is I know so little, and there are such a lot of governesses wanting engagements.   I don't think I'd better try for that, do you ?'

' Well, perhaps there are rather too many incompetent persons in that line of industry,' Thrale observed.

' I could be a nurse, or—or a general servant—only not in Rockingham, Bernard. I should not like that.'

' That is the first point to settle.   We ought to make up our minds in the next half-hour whether you would care to stay in Rockingham under any conditions or not.'

' *Ought* I to stay there ?' she asked, after a few moments' reflection upon the opening duties of her new life.

' That depends upon whether you feel like fighting.'

' Fighting?' she echoed, wondering what line of industry might require ability of that kind in a young woman of her age.

' You see, Denise,' Thrale explained, ' now there is no longer any justifiable reason for leaving society in error, it might be advisable to reveal the whole truth—to stay in the place, and show these scandal-mongers, who have turned their backs upon you when you needed a friend, that they have shamefully wronged you—to stay here until they were forced to acknowledge their injustice and beg your pardon.   That's what I call fighting—and that's what I should do if I were in your place.'

He thrust out his prominent under-jaw, and bent his brows in savage determination. In the past week he had fathomed the mystery easily enough, and learnt why

Denise had been deserted by every friend. For her sake, and in view of Harding's possible return, he had not attempted to undeceive anyone, knowing that if Harding came back the innocence of Denise would be amply shown. So far as he himself was concerned in the scandal, he cared not two pins whether these fools, who were so easily led by mere rumour, held him innocent or guilty. But it was another matter when the reputation of Denise was at stake; and for her sake he was prepared to take up his abode in Rockingham, and prove her innocence by every means that ingenuity and determination could afford.

' I don't feel that I could do that, Bernard,' said Denise presently.

' If you go away, they will say you were afraid to stay.'

' So I am.'

' They will take it as another proof that

you were to blame. Heaven only knows what stories they may not invent. They may say that you were turned adrift for some abominable fault——'

'What does that matter if I have done no wrong?'

'It means that they will do you all the injury they possibly can. There is no limit to the cruelty of civilized society. The barbarians who stoned unhappy women to death were more merciful.'

'But Rockingham is only a little place in the world——'

'On the other hand,' continued Thrale, 'there would be not much difficulty in tackling the Vicar to begin with. He would be bound to make some effort to assert Christian justice. Then there's Mrs. Balfour; we could make her listen——'

'And suppose, Bernard, that we told this horrible story everywhere, and forced everyone to acknowledge that I have done no ill ; what then ? Do you think I want them to pity me ? Oh, that would be more terrible than anything ! If Mrs. Balfour asked me to be her companion again, do you think I could accept ? Oh, no, no, no !'

' It isn't their compassion we want, but it's decent fair play and common honesty,' said Thrale, his jaw standing out more fiercely than ever.

' Bernard, I'm only a weak little woman, remember.'

' That should be a stronger reason for fighting your cause. But it's not. No, you're right ; we must do what is expedient, not what is quixotic ;' and, dropping the glass, he thrust his head out of the window and told the driver to go to the station.

CHAPTER XXII.

EXPEDIENCY.

THE subject was not reopened until they were in the train and on their way to London. But the thoughts of both were occupied in seeking a solution to the difficulties that environed them, Thrale's revolving round his own text—'We must do what is expedient.' At length Denise said timidly :

'If you are going to India, Bernard, and you did not mind, I should like to go there, too.'

He looked at her without speaking, smiling at the idea that he might object to her being near him.

'It would be as easy to find an occupation there as in London, I should think,' she continued.

'I dare say it would; but we must first earn the money to pay for the journey. I am not much richer than you. See'—emptying his purse in one hand and displaying a few sovereigns—'that's all I have.'

'Oh, Bernard, why did you come first-class?'

'I don't mind showing you,' he said, disregarding her question, 'because——' He paused, and, jingling the gold in his hand as he looked at her, asked: 'Do you know anyone in London?'

'Nobody.'

'You haven't a single friend there?'

'Not one.'

'Nor I, so you see there must be a good deal of mutual dependence between us. That's why I thought you ought to know the limits of my funds. We shall have to scrape and economize to rub along until we are earning the living wage.'

' Won't you go to India ?' she asked brokenly.

' Alone !—not I. And what would you do in London without a friend ?'

' But you had an appointment there.'

' That fell through last week. There was another man in the field, and they couldn't wait for me. It's all the same ; I can earn as much in London.'

' But you were so eager to go—so en-thusiastic about India. We couldn't persuade you to give up the idea.'

' I suspect I am capricious. Anyhow, I don't want to go now. Come, let us think of something more serious,' he said abruptly, feeling that Denise was stepping upon dangerous ground, and might conceive the truth, that his eagerness to leave England had been due to consciousness that his love

for her was not otherwise to be overcome.

Detecting the shade of embarrassment on
his face, and misconstruing it, she drew closer
to him, and, laying her hand upon his arm,
said timidly :

'I can't be unselfish just now, Bernard—
not unselfish enough to ask you to go away,
just as if nothing had happened to me. I
know it's for my sake you are staying. It
isn't caprice. You couldn't be capricious.
It's all pity for me. And, oh, I am so grateful ! But after a little while, when I get
better and stronger, I can bear to let you go.'

We will hold together till then,' said he,
with more fervour in his voice than he had
yet permitted himself. 'When I know quite
well that you can do without me, I will go—
but not before.'

She did not perceive the deeper meaning
of his words—love of the kind he felt being

banished from her heart; she saw only the staunch affection of an exceptionally loyal friend.

'It's more than friendship,' she said; 'if you were my brother, you could not be more kind.'

'I've been turning over that idea of a fraternal relationship,' he replied, with a marked absence of enthusiasm. 'It's the only way that I can see of getting over certain difficulties in our way.'

'I don't think I quite understand——'

'You see, Denise,' said he, separating the pieces of gold in his palm with one finger, 'there's only about seventeen pounds here; they wouldn't last long in a hotel—about a week, I should say. Whereas we might live in decent lodgings fairly well on four or five——'

'Oh, less than that,' she said eagerly. 'You don't know how economical I can be.

Oh, Bernard !' She paused, clasping her hands, for the thought of having him with her, of their sharing the same home, brought a gleam of sunshine upon her future, which she feared must presently be overclouded and lost.

'It could be managed if we palmed ourselves off as brother and sister—not otherwise, I'm afraid.'

' But if I feel that you are a brother to me, and if you could think of me as a poor unhappy little sister, is there any harm in it ? No one is any the worse for thinking we are related.'

' We'll try it, anyhow,' said he more cheerfully, and with resolution. Then he slipped a few sovereigns into his pocket, and putting the rest of the money back in the purse, gave it to Denise, telling her it was for her house-keeping expenses. She took the money without remonstrance, only wondering sadly why the project of living with her as a brother was repugnant to him. For she knew he must love her, and with all a brother's affection.

He also asked himself why the notion was so distasteful. To meet her when he came from his room in the morning, to spend his hours of leisure with her, to bring a smile back to her face from time to time—these were the dearest desires of his heart.

Was it merely his hatred of falsehood in any shape, his scorn of expedient as a cowardly evasion of responsibilities, that created this unpleasant feeling? He thought it must be that. For the possibility of divorcing Harding and of making Denise his wife had not yet occurred to him. Had any idea of that kind presented itself to his mind, his feeling would have revolted against it as an outrage upon delicacy.

This was a season of mourning for him

equally with Denise; they had yet to bury their dead, yet to forget their all-absorbing grief, before they could foster thoughts of love.   But for all that, at the root of his discontent was the fear that he could never be anything more than a brother for Denise.

CHAPTER XXIII.

THE CHANGE IN DENISE.

By the end of the week Thrale and Mrs. Harding—they thought it advisable to drop her title now—were comfortably installed in a pleasant suite of rooms upon Putney Common.

'To-morrow,' said Thrale on Sunday, 'I shall go out and look for work.'

'I think I can make my dress and things in a week,' said Denise; 'then *I* must begin to look about for employment.'

'You'll never stand in need of employment while I'm in the house; I want such a lot of things, and never know where to find what I want. When we can afford to keep a house-keeper and a couple of servants, it will be soon enough for you to turn out of a cold morning, and drudge all day, and come home fagged out at night.'

' But our money, Bernard——'

' Don't you know the proverb?—any fool can make money, but it needs a wise person to spend it. I'll make the money, and you shall spend it, and save and save and save to your heart's content. And in that way, with the content of doing our best, we must grow rich beyond the dreams of avarice, contentment being a blessing that avarice never can dream of.'

It was late when he came home the following evening, but he carried a bundle under his arm, and was in high spirits.

' There's a week's work to begin with, and more to follow. No ; it's not washing,' he said, as Denise touched the packet inquisitively. 'I'll tell you all about it when I've had something to eat.'

'Are you hungry?' asked Denise, ringing the bell.

'As a hunter should be. And if I weren't, your table would make me hungry. Why, where did you get your flowers?'

'In Putney. I got all these, and those on the chimney, for fourpence.'

He declared they were worth four shillings, and then, looking about him, fell to admiring everything silently as he pulled off his gloves —the table laid with scrupulous care, the glasses glittering brightly—he knew she must have given them an extra polish with one of her new dusters—the sprays of flowers here and there, the glowing fire—and never a cinder on the hearth—the easy-chairs drawn round towards the fire, suggestive of a long after - dinner gossip ; and lastly his eyes rested upon Denise as she brought him a pair of new slippers that had been toasting on the fender for the past two hours, and, seeing a happy smile in her face, he breathed a long sigh of contentment.

'And now tell me what is in the parcel,' Denise said, when his appetite was somewhat appeased.

'Manuscripts. Oh, I've been wonderfully lucky; and this is a day to be pricked out on the calendar. Happened to fall upon just the right sort of man—which was the more delightful because I had previously dropped on five or six of the other sort—Knight, of ——, the big publisher. A man after my own heart, clear-sighted, bold, and kindly; a man who looks you straight in the eyes, and makes up his mind there and then whether you are to be trusted or not. Exceptional men take unusual courses. He had written to me once expressing his approval of certain critiques on his firm's books which appeared in the *Herald*. They were honest critiques, I'll say that for them. And when I introduced myself this afternoon as the writer of those articles, and asked for employment as a reader, he offered me half a dozen manuscripts to read and report upon for a fee of half a guinea each, short and long. You may be sure I said snap, and there they are.'

'Then, you won't have to go away every day ? you can read them here ?'

'If I may.'

'Oh, that is beautiful ! You shall have this room, and I can work in the little room.'

'I prefer the small room, if it's all the same to you. Genius wants a lot of tobacco-smoke, and wants it thick.'

When he came down the next morning, he found that Denise had prepared the small room for his use. A fire was burning brightly ;

a table and chair were placed in the very best position for light and warmth ; his pipes and tobacco held an important place beside the pile of MSS. ; and a narcissus stood in a glass to gratify his eye. Denise stood with twinkling eyes, pleased with her effort to please him. Turning to her, he said tenderly :

'You are awfully good, *dear*.'

The word escaped him unconsciously. Many a time it had risen to his lips and been repressed ; but the impulse just now took him off his guard.

She smiled gently. The term of endearment was grateful to her ear. Why should they repress sweet words if they really felt towards each other the tender love of brother and sister ? It was quite natural and right. One day he would kiss her, and that would make her happier still. She would know then, indeed, that he loved her as his

sister — loved her as much as she loved
him.

He began work that morning in the little
room.   He did what he called tough stuff
here.   But often he would bring a manuscript in the sitting-room, and read it aloud to
Denise while she worked.   He had the true
scent of a born critic, and at a glance could
tell if the work was readable and pleasant,
or not.

' You've only to thrust a paper-knife in the
middle and sniff it, to know whether the stuff
is good or bad,' said he.

Those were pleasant times for Denise—
the pleasantest possible for one in such a
position as hers.   Her thoughts could not
stray away when he read, as they would
when she was simply cutting out or stitching
alone.   He read well, and compelled attention by sometimes breaking off to ask her
opinion on a certain passage, or to discuss

some doubtful point, declaring that she could see straight to the root of a thing while he was wandering amongst its branches, and so made her feel that she was actually of use, and some sort of a helpmate.

To him these days were pregnant with such happiness as he had never before known.   It was no longer a Dead Sea fruit that played before his hungering eyes, but a rich growth, as sweet as it was beautiful, ripening surely to its full perfection.

Sometimes, when she had bidden him good-night, he would thrust aside his 'tough stuff,' reserved for night-work, and, turning to the fire, would light a pipe and dream of the future.   And now it was that the thought of a divorce came, not indelicately, into his mind.   It was absurd that Denise should be tied for life to a stone.   In a few months' time, perhaps in a few weeks, it might be suggested to her that she should free herself from the man who had proved himself utterly unworthy of her consideration. And after that, though Denise might not love him as she had loved Harry, she could yet in time consent to become his wife, if only to put an end to this sham, which must prevent them forming any friendships with other men and women of their own class. But he hoped for something more than that ; he hoped that her affection would ripen into such a passion as he himself felt for her, and trusted to the effect of time and her healthy organism for this result. A long time, he knew, must elapse before the memory of Harding could be effaced, before her stricken heart recovered its normal faculties, and her nature yearned for the fulfilment of its natural functions. But he was in no hurry ; he had so long kept his feelings under restraint that he could trust himself not to be betrayed into any premature declaration of his passion,

knowing that, if his feeling was not recipro-
cated, and Denise felt she could not become
his wife, they must put an end at once to
the present arrangement, which was such a
happy one for both, and separate, to the loss
of each.   He preferred that the development
of love on her side should be gradual, and
come within the natural course of events,
rather than it should be forced to a measure
which might take the form of self-sacrifice,
from a sentiment of gratitude on her side.

The result seemed to him assured, if only
Denise could recover perfect bodily health,
the physical strength to meet the moral strain
which had yet to be borne.   He saw that her
cheerfulness was mainly assumed, that many
hours of agony were concealed, for his peace
of mind.   Her wan face and sunken eyes in
the morning showed only too clearly the
suffering of the long night. Could she sustain
this effort ?   Must there not come a time when

exhausted nature should call for repose, and her faculties succumb to the unnatural pressure put upon them ?

With these fears ever on his mind, Thrale watched his companion with intense anxiety, concealing his solicitude for fear of precipitating a climax.   He saw her once, when she believed herself unobserved, press her hand upon her heart, and bow her head in pain.   On another occasion her hand trembled to such a degree that she almost let fall the breakfast-cup she was taking from him ; her lips were livid ; beads of perspiration stood upon her temples, and she abruptly left the room.

Then, on Sunday, as he was reading aloud the last of the week's MSS., he was suddenly dismayed by hearing a faint cry, and before he could render her assistance, Denise had slid from her chair, and lay to all appearance dead upon the floor.   He rang the bell violently, and applied such means of restoring life as he could think of. When she returned to consciousness, she was unable to explain the cause of her fainting ; she had only felt a sudden pain—at her heart ; that was all, and it was nothing. Thrale would have gone at once for a doctor, but she entreated him so earnestly not to do so that he refrained, upon her promising to see him if she were again attacked. She seemed quite herself the next morning—so well that Thrale left her after lunch to take his week's work to the publishers and get more.

Denise watched him as far as the end of the street ; then, having put on her coat and hat, she walked into the Richmond Road, where she remembered having seen a red lamp over a doorway, and a brass plate on the gate, with Dr. Somebody engraved upon it. And now, finding the house, she rang the bell timidly, and asked to see the doctor.

The interview that followed was not a long one, but it marked a new era in the life of Denise.

She said nothing about this visit to Thrale, for it was a subject that she could not talk about even to her brother.

' I am quite, quite well,' she said in answer to the earnest inquiry with which he greeted her on his return ; and holding his hand in hers, she looked in his face with unwonted animation as she continued : ' I am not going to be foolish again.   I won't make you anxious about myself any more, my poor Bernard.'

Indeed, a noticeable improvement dated from that day—a change so great that it perplexed Thrale.   No effort was necessary now for her to take interest in ordinary topics.   On the contrary, she seemed at times to be holding fluttering excitement under control, and the apathy of previous days was replaced by subdued vivacity. Her busy fingers were never idle; it delighted Thrale, looking up from his work, to observe the look of concentration and strenuous energy in her face as she plied the needle. But he put his veto on working after dinner, with the result that on going late to bed one night, and pausing by her door, he heard the rapid click of the needle within. The next morning he remonstrated with her.

'I must get that horrid frock done and out of the way,' she said.

'But you said it was for spring, and that is still far ahead. And it's horrible to think of you sitting in the cold working as if it were for life.'

'I like the cold; but I won't work in my room if you don't like it.'

He bound her to that promise, but the work was more engrossing than ever in the sitting-room. One day, when he entered abruptly from his room, she huddled the work up in her lap with a cry of alarm, and laughingly begged him to go back to his den again only for one minute. What on earth was she at now ? he wondered.

She astonished him one night, when they were sitting before the fire, by opening the subject of divorce, after a little interval of silence, and quite irrelevantly to the matter they had been discussing.

'I don't think a woman ought ever to give up the hope of reclaiming a husband who has left her. For her children's sake,' she added, by way of explanation, as Thrale made no response to the proposition.

'But if she have no children?' suggested he.

She made no answer to that, and he promptly turned the subject.

Yet it recurred to his mind more than once, and he wondered what she could have been revolving in her little head before she made the observation. It was not long before he found the clue to that and other little mysteries which had puzzled him in the past five or six days.

Needing a pair of scissors to cut out an extract, he went one morning into the next room to borrow them from Denise. She had just left the room to give orders to her landlady about dinner ; so, finding no one there, Thrale lifted the lid of the work-table to help himself.

'What in the name of wonder can this be?' he asked himself, taking up a very diminutive garment in cambric. For a moment he thought that Denise must be dressing a doll for her landlady's child ; and then light suddenly flashed upon his clouded masculine mind, the thing being too big for a doll—it was for a baby.

CHAPTER XXIV.

DENISE PLAYS HER CARD.

THAT look of concentration and energy of purpose in Denise's face was not without significant result. When business again took Thrale to the City, she profited by his absence to find her way to Lincoln's Inn. There she was fortunate enough to find Mr. Playfair.

'I am most happy to see you, madam,' said the little lawyer when Denise was seated in his sanctum. 'For the past fortnight we have been endeavouring by every possible means to learn your address——'

'Does my husband want to see me?' asked Denise eagerly.

'No, madam; we have not had the pleasure of receiving any communication from Sir Henry; but, in justice to our client, we are most anxious to conclude this affair in the manner he desired. In fact, we feel hardly justified in making any definite disposition of his estate until your claim is settled, either' (ticking the points off on his thumb and forefinger) 'by your signed agreement to renounce all pecuniary indemnity—the verbal intimation conveyed to us by our Mr. Benson—or by fixing a reasonable estimate in round figures of the maintenance to which you feel yourself entitled.'

'I want to settle that question personally with my husband.'

'That, madam, I fear, is quite out of the question.'

'I *must* see him. There are grave reasons —reasons which he is unaware of.'

'I shall be happy to represent them to our

client; but I can offer you no hope that any advice on our part will induce him to see you.'

Denise reflected for a moment or two, and then, producing a letter she had written to Harry, pouring out her soul with such fervid eloquence as comes to the most simple at such times in an appeal to him to return to the right path, not for her sake, but for the honour of the child which must bear his name, she gave it to Mr. Playfair, and asked when she might expect an answer.

'Well, I should say in about a week's time.'

'Then, he is not in England,' she said sharply.

'I make no admission, Lady Harding; the law is tedious, you know.' He displayed all his false teeth in a smile intended to charm her thoughts from that admission he had made. 'And even if our client were in the next street, I could not undertake to obtain his answer to this important letter without due consideration. I promise you this : it shall be forwarded without delay, and if you will kindly give me your address——'

'No; I will come again next Monday,' said Denise, and then, though Mr. Playfair made a movement as if to close the interview, she sat thinking hard for a minute or two. She was no longer a girl ; she was a woman, and with the probability of becoming a mother, she felt she must be very careful about worldly things, and do nothing foolish.

'Have you sold Harding Court ?' she asked presently.

'Not yet. We are pushing the matter forward, however. Our surveyors have sent in their report ; an inventory has been made of all the furniture and effects in the house, and we have arrived at an approximate valuation of the estate.'

'Will you please tell me how much the Court, with all that it contains, is valued at ?'

' I think I may give *you* that information, although it is scarcely regular. With the home-farm, park, house, furniture and effects, the value may roughly be set down at fifty thousand pounds.'

' How much does he possess besides that ?' asked Denise, after a moment's reflection.

'Really, madam,' remonstrated Mr. Playfair, ' I must decline to answer that question. I have already overstepped, I fear, the limits imposed by professional confidence. If I can serve you in any other way——' He laid his hand upon the door-handle.

Denise rose, considered well whether she had said all that she intended to say, and then, promising to call the following Monday for the reply to her letter, went her way.

That earnest, passionate letter, written carefully after so much forethought and mental conflict, came duly into the General's hands, was read by him in the smoking of one cigarette, and answered in the smoking of the next.

And so, when Denise came again to Lincoln's Inn, Mr. Playfair was enabled to tell her that his client had written to acknowledge the receipt of her letter, and inform him that, as it contained nothing to change Sir Henry's views or call for further consideration, he must beg that the negotiation should be closed without further waste of time in unnecessary correspondence.

She was not unprepared for this answer, but its cold cruelty shocked her and stirred up all the bitter resentment of which her sweet nature was capable. That she should have knelt at the feet of this man, who had proved himself so heartless and wicked, that she should have broken down her pride, obliterated the memory of the wrongs she had endured, overcome her self-respect, humbled herself in the dust as if she were craving pardon for herself rather than opening a way for his redemption, and for this unmanly and inhuman wretch, whose debased soul was dead to honour, to duty, to purity— dead even to the tenderest appeal in nature, the voice of his own child! Oh, it was shameful and degrading!

With these thoughts surging upwards for utterance, she would not trust herself to speak after the lawyer had delivered his heartless message, but sat with bent head and lips tightly pressed, as if to repress the words that must betray her husband's dishonour, whilst he sorted his papers noiselessly, regarding her from the corner of his eye.

'I think,' he observed quietly, after a time, and still fingering his papers—'I think we must take this letter as final, Lady Harding, the ultimate decision on our client's part.'

Denise drew a long sigh as she raised her head and turned to the lawyer.

'Yes, yes,' said she; 'I have done all that I will—all that I can do.'

'In that case,' said he with alacrity, taking a dip of ink and flourishing his quill over a quire of foolscap, 'we may be able to settle at once the question between us.'

'Yes; I have made up my mind how much I must have.'

'I am most delighted to hear it. Now,' taking another dip and another flourish, 'now, what shall we say, in round figures?'

'Fifty thousand pounds,' replied Denise without hesitation.

The roundness of these figures took Mr. Playfair's breath away.

'You are not speaking seriously, madam, surely. Perhaps, under the influence of momentary irritation, you are disposed to assess your claim at a higher figure than you would upon calmer consideration.'

'No; I have been thinking about it all

the week, and that is the sum I demand.'

' But fifty thousand pounds, my dear Lady Harding, think ! It's an enormous sum of money.'

'I'm very sorry,' said Denise—and she really seemed to regret the pain she was giving the little gentleman — ' very sorry indeed ; but I could not possibly do with less.'

Mr. Playfair laid down his pen and joined his thumbs, reflectively shaking his head. Denise wore the plain hat and coat she had bought as being more suitable to her present condition than the rich fur-trimmed mantle and bonnet in which she had left the Court. Why such a plain little person could not do with less than this sum perplexed him.

' Have you considered that the interest upon this sum at five per cent. gives an annual income of two thousand five hundred pounds? Now, allowing for your position and the cost of living, do not you think you might make, say, a thousand a year do? That would be a sum down of twenty thousand——'

'Oh no; I couldn't possibly do with anything less!'

'Well, madam, you must allow me to communicate again with our client, for, although I am instructed to close with any reasonable demand, I should not feel justified in settling the case at such a cost as you indicate.'

'Then, what am I to do?' asked Denise.

'In the first place, you must allow us another week to obtain instructions from our client, and then, if his reply proves unsatisfactory, I should advise you to take the advice of a solicitor.'

Denise rose, thanking Mr. Playfair, and promised to act upon his advice.

The next letter from Harding's solicitor that fell into the General's hand drew a long whistle from his lips.

'Fifty thousand! Why, that's about half the estate. Greedy little beggar! Fifty thou.—a modest demand, upon my word, Madame Denise! Well,' thought he, after a restorative nip of cognac, 'I don't blame her for feathering her nest, and I don't think I begrudge it her, either, for she deserves her share in the plucking of the pigeon.'

CHAPTER XXV.

DENISE astonished Thrale one Monday evening at the close of the month by asking if he knew of any solicitor in their neighbourhood.

'A solicitor, Denise?' he exclaimed. 'Why, what scheme are you working out now in that busy little brain of yours?'

'I want to buy Harding Court, that's all. Only I don't see how I am to buy it myself.'

'I should think not. First of all, you have to find the money.'

'I've got that, dear,' said she, with a triumphant little nod; and, opening her purse, she drew out the cheque she had received that morning from Mr. Playfair.

Thrale examined it with increased amazement.

' Why, when did you receive this, and who gave it you?' he asked.

Then she told him of the steps she had taken, which she had concealed from him at first from motives of delicacy—the cause was now no longer a secret between them— and afterwards from the fear that it might come to nothing, and so create solicitude on his part without reason.

' But it was all settled this morning,' she said in conclusion; 'and when I told Mr. Playfair what I intended to do with the money, he said he should be happy to negotiate—that's the word—negotiate with my solicitor.'

' You wonderful little woman!' said he, regarding her with warm admiration, for his imagination readily supplied the details in this transaction which she, from modesty, suppressed. 'And what are you going to do with the Court when it's bought?'

'Of course I don't think of living there ; that would be foolish. And, oh, I wouldn't change this little home for that great house, not for all the riches in the world, unless——' she paused, twisting her fingers within each other, as was her habit when uneasy speculations came into her mind.

'I know,' he said, waiving the subject. 'Do you know how much the Court will cost?'

'All that, I think—fifty thousand pounds !' He nodded, and was silent in thought.

'Not alone,' she continued, reverting to her former train of thought—'nor even with my dear brother—I couldn't live there. It isn't for myself, dear. But I thought that if anything happened to me it would be a provision for the—the little one. And I thought

that I ought to do this when *he* showed so
clearly that he had no care at all what became
of either of us. And I thought,' she pro-
ceeded, with a little wavering in her voice,
'that, if it should be a son, it would encourage
him to work very hard and make a fortune,
thinking the Court would be his ; and one day
he might go to live there, and win every-
body's love, and restore the honour of the
family that has flourished there so long.'

Thrale saw the tears of pride, and hope,
and joy, springing in her eyes, but dimly, for
the moisture gathered in his own, his heart
being touched with love and sympathy.

'It will cost a good deal to keep up,' he
said huskily, to turn the subject.

'I have thought of that, Bernard,' she
said, her newly-born business instinct pricking
into activity. 'Evans, who rents the ten-
acre farm, offered quite a great deal—I think
it was a hundred and fifty a year—for the

home-farm, which joins on, you know. And I should say that would pay for repairs and things.'

Thrale nodded.

'I'll hunt up a solicitor to-morrow,' said he.

'You see, dear,' said Denise, after a pause, drawing a little nearer to him, and laying her hand on his arm, 'there's no knowing what may happen. Perhaps, if he'—she could not bring herself to name her husband otherwise —'if he is led away by bad people, and spends all his money, and is deserted by them, he may one day be glad to come back to us.'

'That is not unlikely,' said Thrale; and then they both looked into the fire in silence and thought.

He knew well enough now that this noble little lady by his side could never be nearer to him than now—a sister, and no more. He had been a fool to dream anything other,

and had wronged her devotion and steadfast,
clear-sighted conscience by conceiving that
she would ever give up the hope of reclaiming her husband. And already she foresaw
the inevitable end—the return of the ruined
blackguard whining for mercy ; and she
would show mercy who had received none
and be generous and self-sacrificing to the
very end.

Could nothing be done to help this brave
little woman—to ameliorate her fate by only
one degree ? Must Harding sink to the
lowest depth of infamy before he could be
taken back by his wife ? If he could only
now be set upon his legs, morally, the case
would not be so wretchedly hopeless. Thrale
thought that if he could only get hold of him
for an hour he might yet do something with
him. 'If it were only to give him a d——d
good parting kick, it would be something!
thought he, shoving out his lower jaw.

'You've never had a word from that old rascal Gordon, I suppose?' he said at length.

Denise shook her head.

'Don't know where he is to be found?'

'I—I think he said he was going to Monte Carlo.'

'That's it!' said Thrale, slapping his knee. 'I warrant he's there gambling with somebody else's money. You told me, I think, that it took a week to get a reply to your letter.'

'Yes, dear. Why?'

'If the General's at Monte Carlo, I feel pretty sure he's got Harding with him.'

'But he slipped away in the General's absence.'

'Never mind about that. It's just possible the old man found him again. Any way, it might be worth while finding out.'

'Would it be of any use to write to him at

Monte Carlo, with the chance of the letter reaching him ?'

'None at all, I should say,' answered Thrale, knowing that if the General were there with Harding any intimation of their suspicions would only cause him to decamp at once.

'Do you think, dear, I ought to go there ?' Denise asked, when she had overcome the repugnance which she felt at the first prospect of such an expedition.

'No. It's a forlorn hope at the best—the barest chance of taking them by surprise and matching craft by craft—an enterprise which I could not suffer you to undertake, even if there were a reasonable hope of succeeding. You have done enough in all conscience—more than enough ; it's my turn to do something.'

'It would take time and cost a great deal, wouldn't it, dear ?'

'Not more than we can afford.   Less than
we would give for the peace of mind it would
yield us to feel that we had left no stone
unturned.   And if even at the eleventh hour
we could rescue him——'

'Oh, if we could!'

'We will think about it, Denise; a day or
two's delay can make no difference.'

She took his hand and held it, pressing it
gently, in recognition of his dear brotherly
love, for she knew that he had made up his
mind to go before he allowed himself to
suggest the possibility.

On Wednesday he started for the Riviera,
with all his travelling requisites in a hand-bag
that was already half filled with the manuscripts he took to read on the journey.   At
the last moment Denise put a letter in his
hand, saying it was the only part she could
take in the Forlorn Hope.   To his surprise,

Thrale found that it was addressed, not to her husband, but to the General. Personal inquisitiveness was the least attribute of his nature, yet Thrale wondered more than once what argument Denise could bring to bear upon the time-serving old scamp.

Recollecting several instances of her reticence with regard to him, her invariable silence when he had expressed his opinion in outspoken terms upon the General's shifty and untrustworthy character, he was disposed to think that she still believed him to be a gentleman, and her friend. Was this an appeal to his friendship in the name of her dead father? he asked himself. Probably it was.

About five o'clock on Friday afternoon he arrived at Monte Carlo. Leaving the Casino and the great hotels behind him, he worked his way towards Monaco till he found a hotel more in harmony with his limited resources. There he took a room, and, having refreshed himself with a wash and a fairly good dinner, he set out for the Casino with such feelings as many another experiences whose fate may be decided by the chances of that establishment.

A train from Nice was just in, and a crowd of visitors were streaming in by the broad steps. He joined them; left his hat and overcoat in the cloak-room, obtained a card of entrance to the gaming-rooms at the office opposite, and passed into the spacious atrium. A compact crowd waited at the entrance to the Salle de Théâtre; a scattered throng of well-dressed men, with a sprinkling of over-dressed women, were sauntering up and down.

Thrale ran his eye over the crowd with little expectation of finding either the General or Harding there, and made his way to the gaming-room. At the entrance he asked the man who inspected his entrance card if he had seen General Gordon enter, on the chance of his being a well-known habitué.

'Général Gordon,' repeated the man reflectively ; and then, with a shrug and an amicable smile, he added : ' Mon Dieu!   Il y a tant des Générals.'

It was a busy night at the Casino ; the players stood four deep round the roulette-tables ; the hot atmosphere was charged with an odour peculiar to these rooms—the smell of greasy bank-notes, cosmetiques, and stale scents.   Above the hushed murmur of the crowds rose the metallic click of gold and silver under the croupiers' rakes, the rattle of the ivory ball in the roulette, and the monotonous call of the chefs, ' Faites vos jeux, messieurs ; rien ne va plus,' and the numbers which disposed of a fortune at each coup.

Thrale took the tables systematically, scanning carefully the serried faces of the players that surrounded one, and then passing on to the next. It took him over an hour to get through the roulette-rooms. Coming to the Grande Salle, where trente-et-quarante alone is played, the task became easier, the players being comparatively few; yet here it was easy to overlook even a well-known face amongst the continually shifting outer ranks of players, and it was difficult to get a fair view of those seated at the table. Indeed, he had come to the last table, and in despair was thinking of going back to the roulette-rooms and beginning all over again, when he heard a well-known voice just in front of him say ' Assuré,' and, craning forward, he recognised the General's long, hooked nose and white moustache as he pushed a piece across to the croupier.

Thrale drew a long breath, and, working

his way to the opposite side of the table,
found a better point of observation. It was
he, the General, beyond a doubt, and looking
remarkably well, his dark hair lustrous with
health and hairwash, his white moustache
looking more princely now for a Russian
twirl. He was in correct evening dress, and
a superb diamond glittered upon his finger.
Piles of five-louis pieces served as paper-
weights to a couple of bulky packets of notes,
and he had a gold pin to prick off results
upon his card. The coolness with which he
saw his five notes of a thousand francs raked
into the bank three times in succession was
only equalled by the indifference with which
he added twenty notes of the same value to
his stock on the fourth coup. He was in
fine fettle, magnificent, and Thrale, in despite
of himself, could not help admiring the old
vagabond.

But where was his pigeon, Harding, who

must, at least, have given the needy General
the means of starting upon this royal road?
Thrale examined every face at the table with
scrupulous care, and then, having no anxiety
with regard to finding the General again,
left him, and passed the other tables under
review.

'He'll never look as he did,' thought he
with a pang; but he could find no man that
bore any resemblance to Harding, nor any
woman that looked like Liz.

So at length, giving up his quest, he went
back and kept his eye on the General. A
little after ten the General looked at his
watch, put up his notes and card in a case,
slipped the gold in his pocket, and rose from
the table. With his thumbs in his waistcoat
pockets, his head well up, and an amiable
eye for the handsome women in his passage,
the General was sauntering towards the
entrance, when Thrale, coming to his side,

his square, protruding chin well in evidence, said :

'Good-evening, General.'

The General, pulling up sharply with a kind of who-the-deuce-are-you look, faced Thrale for a moment, and then, recognising him, took his hand, held it stiffly, drawing back as if to show all the world that he was not ashamed to acknowledge a friend, however humble, and gave it two hearty shakes, saying in his deepest and chestiest voice :

'My dear boy! This is indeed an un-expected delight, and an ample compensa-tion for a deuced bad night. But whoever expected to see you here? I thought you gentlemen of the press, whilst very careful to give the latest betting at Newmarket, usually condemn this honest establishment as a sink of iniquity.'

'Our practice, General, usually runs counter

to our theory,' observed Thrale, who was prepared to make himself agreeable—to descend, in fact, to the most jesuitical expedient for the sake of Denise.

CHAPTER XXVI.

THE GENERAL FINESSES.

'WHERE are you staying, my dear chappie?' asked the General, taking Thrale's arm as they descended the Casino steps.

'Hôtel du Midi.'

'Hôtel du Midi! That's odd. *I* know it well. Alone?'

'Yes.'

'No engagement to-night?'

'None.'

'Then you must consider yourself my prisoner.'

'Willingly.'

Thrale did not intend to lose sight of the

General if he could help it until he had
solved the question that had brought him
so far.

'I am staying at the Hôtel de Paris, just
across the *place* there.   The charges are
stiffish, you know ; but it's exceedingly convenient, and the *chef* is a *cordon bleu*.   We
will have a nice little supper, and then, with
a cigar on the terrace, afterwards we can talk
over certain matters that are the fly in my
pot of precious ointment.   We won't spoil
our appetite by discussing serious subjects
now.   So you've been saying at the Hôtel
du Midi, dear boy ?'

'I arrived this afternoon.'

'Oh, oh!' thought the General—'didn't
lose much time in hunting me up.   I see
your game.   What a strange thing!' said he
at the same time.   'That's the very place I
pitched upon when I first arrived.   To tell
you the truth, dear boy'—dropping his voice

to a whisper—'I was in a fearsome pickle. Hadn't ten pounds to change at the bureau, I give you my word, and that wasn't my own.   You see, that poor miserable beggar had made me paymaster, and when he eloped he left a balance of about twenty pounds in my hands.   Half of that went in hunting about for him in London and getting here. With the remainder I began punting five-franc pieces at roulette—a detestable, degrading business—dirty little shopkeepers, fat Jewesses, seedy riff-raff of all sorts, reaching over your head, breathing garlic into your face, scrambling for their money like dogs for a bone, quarrelling, pilfering, and smelling—— Pah!   Well, I had to put up with that.   Couldn't afford to go in for a system, you know — you understand the tables——'

'Not a bit,' replied Thrale in a tone that implied 'and I don't want to.'

'Ah, ah!' thought the General. 'Obviously he hasn't come here to play. All right !' And he said : ' Nearly all are forms of the Martingale ; but I dared not venture even on the " Simple Philibert," so I played on zero.'

'What's that ?'

'Simplest thing in the world, dear boy ! The roulette is divided into thirty-seven compartments, each numbered from zero upwards. The ball is bound to fall into one of those holes. On an average the ball falls into zero every thirty-seventh coup. Then the bank has to pay the winner thirty-six pieces for every one he has on—see ? My plan was to wait until the twentieth coup after zero had won. The ball may tumble in the very first time, in which you make a clear profit of thirty-five pieces. If it doesn't you lose your piece and stake another, and so on until it does win. Beginning at twenty, it is exceedingly rare that you can lose thirty times before zero wins ; but if you do, your gain is still six pieces. As I tell you, I began with a single piece of five francs ; but I was lucky, and at the end of the week I could afford to put on four at each time, and so I crept on until a week ago, when I was in a position to turn my back on that perspiring crowd of little punters, and go into the respectable rooms and play in the society of gentlemen. And now, dear chappie, I've got hold of a system—— Well, you shall know all about it presently.   Here we are.'

The hall porter flung the doors open on seeing the General and Thrale, another attendant came forward to take their hats and coats, while a third brought some letters from the bureau for M. le Général.

' I wager three out of these five are begging letters.   Will you take me, dear boy ?' asked the General, offering the unopened letters. ' Not on—wise on your part—you've no idea

what a lot of that sort of thing goes on here.
Oh, Jules,' presenting the letters—of which
one, as he perceived, was actually from Liz—
and turning to the hall porter, 'you will send
up to the Hôtel du Midi for Mr. Thrale's
luggage—arrange the affair—and if the room
next to mine is unoccupied, Mr. Thrale will
use it while he is my guest.'

'The orders of M. le Général shall be
obeyed.'

Thrale submitted to this arrangement : not
that he had any hope now of finding Harding
here. Indeed, so completely had the General's
unconstrained behaviour disarmed him, that
he began to think the old fellow was playing
honestly for once in his life. He was never
more in error.

With the nice refinement of a man who
respects a delicate repast, the General avoided
the discussion of lengthy topics, serious
matter, and even the all-engrossing theme at

Monte Carlo—rouge-et-noir—during supper.
Drawing out his companion, as much as it
was possible with one so moody, taciturn,
and hard to draw as Thrale, he kept up a
running conversation, seasoned with plea-
santries, upon such trifles as harmonized
with the light dishes and the sparkling wine.

It was only when they were seated in the
moonlight on the terrace, with a shaded lamp
that never flickered in the still air, lighting
the facets of a dozen cut caraffes and glasses
on the table between them, with the scent of
lemon-blossom and a thousand flowers float-
ing up from the gardens below, and with an
exquisite cigar in his lips, that the General,
expelling a cloud of smoke with a deep sigh,
said :

'Now, old chappie, you must tell me what
you know about that poor beggar Harding,
and his dear, good little wife.'

'I know nothing about him.'

'I was afraid so. Do you know, dear boy, it struck me just now that perhaps you had come down here to look for him ?'

'I have.'

'No go,' said the General, with a melancholy shake of the head; 'he knew *I* was coming here.'

'A suspicion of that fact led me to believe he would be found at Monte Carlo,' replied Thrale bluntly.

'I wish your conclusions were justified, with all my heart. There would be some hope for the poor old Johnnie then. Why, dear boy, I've seen men here hopelessly entangled, tottering on the very edge of social destruction, all for some pretty doll with a painted face—mad, positively mad. Well, they have gone into the Casino, lost a few thousands, and that's brought them to their senses. Away goes the doll—and they're cured.'

'And they go back to their innocent wives,' thought Thrale bitterly, 'and are forgiven ; and one's the hero of a farcical comedy, and the other the heroine of life's tragedy.'

'Ah,' continued the General, 'you moralists magnify the small iniquities of this place, which any sane man must see are not a patch upon the rascality connected with your sacred turf, nor one-thousandth part so destructive to the general community, and you lose sight altogether of the many advantages derived from it by a deserving section of society.'

Saying this, the General thrust out his legs, tilted back his chair, and, plunging his hands into his pockets, turned over the thick, heavy five-louis pieces lovingly.

CHAPTER XXVII.

ANOTHER TRICK TO THE GENERAL.

'It has occurred to me,' said the General to Thrale, when they met the next morning at breakfast, 'that if Harding is here we ought to find his name in the visitors' lists.' He broke off to order a waiter to fetch *all* the local papers in. 'When I am at the tables (and I do my two *séances* regularly) I see nobody but the chef and the croupiers, so it's not impossible that he is here.'

The garçon brought about as many papers as he could carry.

'Good. Set them down there. Now fetch me the *Indicateur de la Riviera.* That,' he explained to Thrale, 'is a sort of directory published every month, and comprises a list of visitors at all the stations between Cannes and Vintimille. We will go through the lot methodically presently.'

And this colossal task he attacked after breakfast with the greatest equanimity, and certainly with less despondency than Thrale. They found no Harding at Monte Carlo, but the General spotted out a Miss Harding at Villefranche, a Barclay Harding at Nice, a Mrs. Harding and family and suite at Grasse.

'I should try 'em all,' he said. 'There are such lots of misprints in these papers. But before you leave Monte Carlo I should go to the Bureau de Police and make inquiries. The hotels, you know, are compelled to furnish exact lists of all visitors. And then there's the Consul. I'll go with you if you like—he's a capital sort of Johnnie, and will do all he knows to help you.'

'Thanks, I'll call on them,' replied Thrale gloomily. 'I won't trouble you to come; I shall do this ferreting quicker alone.'

'If he's here, or anywhere near here, you must find it out before we meet at lunch.'

Had there been the least prospect of finding Harding, or of discovering treachery on the General's part, Thrale would not have scrupled to avail himself of Gordon's hospitality. But he saw no ground for hope in any direction.

'Thanks again,' said he; 'but I don't think you will see me again.'

'Dear boy,' said the General impressively, dropping his voice, 'permit me to take the liberty of an old friend—how do you stand for cash?'

'I've a hundred francs, that's all.'

'Thought so,' said the General to himself. 'Glad to hear it.' To Thrale he said, in the same genial, earnest tone: 'My dear chappie, you will lunch with me—twelve sharp. After lunch we will go into the Casino for just half an hour.'

'I've no time to lose, nor money either.'

'I promise you shall lose neither. I promise you that you shall win in three hours more than any literary man can make in three years. You shall return to England with a fortune in your pocket——'

'Or to hell, with such as you,' thought Thrale, with some strange instinctive conviction that this apparently harmless old rascal was in truth a fiend possessed of the power to ruin the souls of men and women.

'I have a system,' pursued the General, 'a kind of Martingale——'

That dispelled the uncanny illusion—if illusion it was—and Thrale burst into laughter at the fatuity of the General.

'Why, you all have systems!' he cried. 'And the Casino profits by them. Good heavens, General! don't you know me a little bit ?'

' More than you think, perhaps. Well, dear boy, if you will not suffer me to do the thing more delicately—allow me to offer you this.' And with that he drew the stuffed note-book from his breast-pocket and extended it to Thrale.

' Hang it, sir! what are you thinking about ?' asked Thrale, rising indignantly.

' I am thinking, my dear fellow,' replied the General, unmoved and as bland as before —' I am thinking that, with a hundred francs, you can no more go to Villefranche, Cannes, and Grasse, than you can fly to the moon in search of Harding ; that, with a hundred francs, your inquiries must come to an end in less than a week.'

' Then I must give up the search.'

' No,' said the General in a very low and serious tone.   ' No ; you can't do that if you had—as I must suppose you had—good reasons for believing that Harding is hereabouts. You are bound to pocket your pride —and this,' laying his hand upon the notecase. ' Mr. Thrale, this search is undertaken, not to save Harding, but to serve that poor little wife he has forsaken.' As Thrale made no response, he continued, after a pause : ' You think I have no conscience.'

' I won't flatter you by supposing you overburdened in that particular.'

' No. Nevertheless, I have something within me that serves the same purpose, call it what you please—something that makes me feel more or less satisfied with myself. I don't feel satisfied with myself when I think of Lady Harding.' He paused, leaning forward and looking straight into Thrale's eyes with consummate audacity.

' I don't exactly know what you could have done for her,' Thrale observed.

'It's all right,' thought the General; 'she has not let the cat out of the bag.'

'You might have *tried* to do something, certainly,' added Thrale.

'*That* is exactly what I feel, dear boy. I might have stood by her until my twenty pounds were all gone. What I should have done after that heaven only knows. Certainly I should not be in a position to offer her now this little provision—and that is what my roundabout journey ends in. Hear me out. You told me last night that she is well, and that you know where she is. Take these notes, employ them as you think best in hunting up that poor weak-kneed Harding, or in supplying the personal wants of that poor soul, his wife. I will not take a refusal,' he pursued, as Thrale rose again with emphatic refusal in his look and gesture—'at any rate, you must give my offer consideration. I shall expect to see you at lunch.'

'And if you do not see me,' answered Thrale, ' you will know that no consideration can induce me to take your money, even for Lady Harding.'

The General felt that he had gone dangerously near overdoing it. 'A little more, and he might have taken the money,' he reflected ; ' but I was compelled to pitch it strong. He is pretty sure to tell Denise all about this interview ; she won't see through it. There's no amount of generosity that a woman will not credit you with if you give 'em a fairly plausible reason for it. Keep her in good temper—that's the main thing just now.'

The General lunched alone ; he did not expect for one moment to see Thrale again. But he sent a note to him at the Hôtel du Midi, *after* the last train had left Monte Carlo for Paris, and when the garçon brought it back, with the information that Mr. Thrale was not there, he tipped the man a louis in the fulness of his heart.

He took an early train to Mentone the next morning, to look after his dovecote, as he put it to himself, and make sure that his pigeon was not flown.

CHAPTER XXVIII.

TEMPTED OF THE DEVIL.

FROM the station at Garavan, the General walked to the Villa Bella Vista, a beautiful house surrounded by palms and citrons embedded in flowers, garlanded with roses and gorgeous creepers that twined to the uppermost columns of the belvedere. It stood in the furthermost corner of the Bay of Mentone, where the stream that divides France from Italy falls into the sea. The proprietor, an English lady, having taken a disgust to it after a very disastrous series at Monte Carlo, had readily accepted Harding as her tenant, handing over her servants with the rest of the chattels for the season, at a reasonable price, with the stipulation that the transaction should not be made known to all the world by the visitors' list—a stipulation which the General, who had the arrangement of affairs, most righteously observed.

The General liked exercise in moderation and under agreeable conditions; it steadied his nerves for play; and as he walked along in the generous sunshine, with a sea of liquid jewels on one hand, the olive-clad foot-hills of the Alps on the other, and the white campanile of Bella Vista just showing above the palms and eucalyptus, he experienced that feeling of good-will towards all men which comes with self-contentment.

If he could not make everyone in the world happy, it was only because his means were limited by circumstances over which he had no control. What he most dearly wished

was to make poor Harding happy and comfortable in his present position—so happy
and comfortable that he could never wish to
change it for any other. That note from
Liz, written, doubtless, in a moment of
irritation, to which young women of her
class were only too subject, saying that she
could 'not abear it any longer,' and he must
come home and do something quick, did not
disquiet him greatly; he felt so sure that,
with a little tact, he could do something to
make her life as happy as she wished.

There was a billiard-room in the belvedere.
The windows opening upon the arcade surrounding it were thrown open to let in the
air, fragrant at this hour with heliotrope ; the
pure blue of sky and distant sea was panelled
in a frame of yellow roses and crimson passion-
flowers, twining together on the slender
columns of the arched way. Leaning on
his cue, his chin resting on his hands,

Harding listlessly regarded Liz as she screwed her pliant body about, in the endeavour to make a stroke that might hit something.

'Not that way, my dear.' said the General, entering. 'You can't hope to hit a ball by making a sort of knife-rest of your knuckles in that style. Show her how to hold her hand, Harding.'

Harding did as he was bid, setting his own hand on the board in regular form ; and then, finding that she could not copy, he drew near lethargically, and bent her fingers to the requisite position. At the touch of his hand, the rich blood rushed up to the girl's temples, and she glanced swiftly into his face, her eyes twinkling, as if dazzled with their own brightness. He, as heavy as lead, saw nothing but the set of her fingers, and, having done the best he could, he told her phlegmatically to 'fire away.'

Liz's cue, as might be expected, slid along the side of the ball, and, with a cry of vexation through her set teeth, she stamped her foot upon the floor.

'What a funny chappie you are !' remonstrated the General. 'How can you expect the girl to play if you don't show her how? She's standing right in front of her ball; slant her body round a bit.'

Again Harding did as he was requested, putting his hands upon the girl's waist and shifting her position, all as if it were a tiresome duty; while she, crimson again to the roots of her pretty hair, and quivering with sensibility, bit her under-lip till it was white as her little teeth.

'That's better,' said the General; and he seated himself, with a rest in his hand, to mark the score and keep the game going.

He stayed to lunch with them, and was,

as usual, very chatty and entertaining, relating the latest incidents of the Casino and the current scandal with an enviable lightness of touch and good humour. After lunch he took coffee with them on the terrace, and when his cup was sipped and settled with a glass of liqueur, he found it was time to catch the train, and return to his beloved Monte Carlo.

Leaving them and passing through the salon, he deliberately laid his gloves on the table ; then, descending to the garden, he stood under the terrace and called up to Liz :

'Will you see if I left my gloves in the salon ?' said he, as the girl looked down from above.

'Yes, here they are ; I will bring them down,' she called, understanding now the significant movement of his eyes as he bade her good-bye.

The General met her at the door, and, linking his arm in hers, led her down the path towards the gate.

'Well, what is it, eh, my dear girl?' he asked, with paternal gentleness.

'Why, you see what it is!' she answered fiercely. 'He don't care for me a little bit—he never alters—and I—I—well, I can't bear it any longer!'

'Hum; case of Pygmalion and Galatea reversed.'

'It's no good talking to me about people I don't know!'

'Pygmalion was a sculptor—a man who made images,' he said, bringing himself down to her level. 'And one of these images was life-size and uncommonly good-looking, like you, my dear, and this Johnnie falls madly in love with her——'

'Yes, that's it!' she cried, comprehending the parable. 'It's just like loving and loving a dead thing. Oh, it's maddening ! What became of the gentleman ?'

' He would have gone mad, only he found means to put warmth and life into the image, and then it was all right, you know.'

Liz looked puzzled, taking the case literally, as a fact of to-day.

' I've done all I know,' she said presently. ' I never cross him. If I can think of anything to amuse him, I fetch it. What else can I do ?'

The General cast a sidelong glance at her, raising his eyebrows, and, as that failed to awake her intelligence, he said :

' My dear, if he won't make love to you, you must make love to him.'

Liz regarded him in perplexity for a moment ; then, his meaning becoming suddenly intelligible, she snatched her arm away, and turned her back on him. The General struck a vesta, lit his cigar, and, seeing by a glance over his shoulder that the girl had seated herself on a marble bench with her shoulder turned towards him, he left her to come to her senses, and marched on with a light heart to the station.

Finding him gone, Liz began to hope she had not offended him; for, after all, there was no great harm in what he said, only for the moment it had offended her pride. She had seen ladies carrying flirtations to desperate lengths, and if it was not wrong in them, why should it be wrong in her? Servants and ladies were women all the same. The General had spoken in a friendly way. He was very clever, and, somehow, whatever he did or advised always turned out right in the end. And if it turned Sir Harry from a stone-cold image, like, into a loving man, and put feeling into his heart, would he not be happier and better for it? Oh, for that— to make him loving, and cheerful, and natural

—she would do anything, anything, anything! With these thoughts stirring her blood like strong drink, she started up from her seat and hurried into the house. But before going on to the terrace, she stayed a minute in the salon to overcome the giddiness of this intoxicating passion, and moderate the beating of her heart. Then, before her resolution could fail, she stepped out upon the terrace, to find Harding, with his head sunk in his shoulders. asleep in his chair.

She seated herself silently opposite to him, and leaning forward, her elbows on her knees, and her damp hands glued together, she wondered what it was she loved; why such a passion had sprung out of her compassion for this man. When he lay helpless and broken down in his bed he was interesting, but now he was a mere log, and, with his mouth agape and his cheeks scored with

dull care, not even commonly good-looking.
Liz had had a score of sweethearts in her
time—good-looking, cheerful fellows, most ;
yet she had never felt for one of them one
particle of the passion that throbbed so wildly
in her bosom now.   Many a gentleman
visitor had made her presents, squeezed
her hand on stairs, kissed her in passages,
and even written to her.   She had only to
glance at any man to make a fool of him.
Yet, beyond the mere triumph of making her
fellow-servants laugh at the expense of these
' silly fools,' she had never cared whether she
excited their admiration or not ; but now here
was she ready to lay down her very life for
this one who had never shown a sign of love
for her.   Maybe that was the secret spring
of her passion, his indifference provoking
that craving for the unattainable which is
inherent in our nature.

Suddenly, Harding's head falling back, he

awoke with a snort, and, rubbing his eyes, he looked stupidly about him.

'Anything at the theatre to-night, Liz?' he asked presently, yawning.

'"Madame Favart,"' she answered, her resolution failing utterly under these discouraging conditions.

'Seen it a dozen times. Let's go for a drive'—standing up and stretching himself—'a good long un. I'll go and see about the carriage while you put on your bonnet. Order dinner as late as possible, that's a good girl.'

He hated the evenings and the long nights, when there was nothing to distract his thoughts; when, do what he might—pace the room, plunge his head in cold water, smoke, lie which side he would—back would come the past with its tormenting suggestions of what *might* have been had he only done this or that to keep his wife's love from

straying.   For she had loved him, he knew
that, before they came back from their honeymoon, and fell in again with that cursed false
friend.

They drove to Vintimille and back ; but
somehow Liz failed to find courage to execute
her project—it may have been the necessity
of effort that chilled her.   And after dinner
they strolled along the sea-front, Harding
making the moonlight and the citron-scented
air a pretext for escaping yet another hour
the horror of retrospection, and yet Liz could
not summon the hardihood to put her
thoughts into words, her purpose into action ;
only, when they said good-night in the vesti-
bule, she retained his hand for a moment
after he would have withdrawn it, looking
into his eyes with such fervour in hers that
he could no longer ignore their testimony.
She ran away from him with a little hysterical
laugh, and he looked after her with a curious

awakening of his senses; he noticed the swish of her white-frilled petticoat and the twinkle of her pretty feet as she ran upstairs, and when she reached the landing, he saw her turn boldly round and wait there with a significant smile in her face.   He nodded awkwardly, like a boy, and went out into the garden.

He paced the alleys, thinking now not of the past and its possibilities, but of the present and its facts.   Liz was in love with him—him of all men on the earth!   This, then, was the explanation of many a lingering look and trembling touch that he had attributed to sympathy and pity.   She cared for him in another way, and now some new sentiment with regard to her seemed springing in his breast—something that gave him unwonted interest in her, a feeling of carelessness that had long been unknown.   What if he let this sentiment grow and take the place of morbid regret, putting the past from his

memory and opening up a prospect of indifference and pleasure ? Why should he live
with the dead when the living stood there
with open arms to breathe a fresh life into
his dormant soul ?   Why should he spend
sleepless nights brooding over the lock of
brown hair and the tattered letter of one who
had betrayed him and broken his heart, when
he might sleep and forget, and dread the
night no more ?

He went indoors presently, still feverishly
agitated.   Before the room in which he
usually passed the lone hours, he hesitated.
Should he go in there to-night, and try to
read the book that lost all meaning to him
after the first few paragraphs, where in every
line he seemed to see the name of Denise ; or
should he go upstairs, where he knew Liz
was waiting for him ?   He sickened at the
thought of again going through that bitter
mockery of attempting to forget, and, glanc-

ing at the stairs, his imagination turned to
Liz with a quick sense of relief.

For a minute or two he stood irresolute,
shaken by the undefined conflict of good and
evil principle within him ; then some glimmer-
ing perception of consequences dawning upon
him, his heart sank with a feeling of self-
loathing and disgust, and, pushing the door
open, he entered the solitary room, crying
hoarsely, ' No, no !'

What was it caused this sudden revulsion
of feeling ? Some clinging memory revived
by the vision of tender caresses that conjured
up a chilling comparison of Liz with the wife
to whom he had given all that was in his
heart to give ? Or was it some nobler and
less selfish sentiment, the last flickering light
of honour, of manly regard for the weak, of
chivalrous respect for purity ?

There were writing materials on the table.
He snatched up a pencil, and wrote a few

hurried words to the General, telling him to make a suitable provision for Liz's future, and send her home to her friends in England. In a postscript he intimated that he might be found at Nice when Liz was gone. He put the letter in an envelope, addressed it to the General, and left it where it must be found ; then he went out of the house quickly and away from it—never looking back, lest he might be tempted to return.

When the General came in after midnight, Liz herself gave him the letter, and waited silent and trembling to know what it contained. The General ran his eye over the page, tore off the postscript, and handed the letter to Liz without a word.

'Where is he gone ?' she gasped as the paper dropped from her hand. The General shrugged his shoulders.

'To-morrow,' said he, 'we will look for him at Monte Carlo ;' he had already decided that the easiest way of curing Liz of one passion was to excite another. ' If we don't find him there, we may take it for granted that he has gone back to his wife.'

For a week or so Liz was seen at Monte Carlo, where she attracted a good deal of attention by her prettiness and the bizarre contrast of her demure dress with the feverish recklessness of her play. And then—she disappeared.

Poor Liz! If you have drifted into the sea of lost souls, 'twas by no fault of the man you loved so passionately. If you still live, you must think kindly of him who would not do you wrong!

CHAPTER XXIX.

THE ROAD TO DESTRUCTION.

WHEN Liz was no longer in the Villa Bella Vista, to make life endurable, a substitute had to be found, to prevent Harding going melancholy mad or blowing his brains out in sheer desperation. The substitutes proposed by the General were all rejected by Harding : he himself proposed the remedy.

'Play seems to agree with you,' said he. 'I'll try how it goes with me.'

The General reluctantly admitted that he knew of no better means for curing a man of morbid sentiment. The idea had occurred to him long ago ; but the practical application he postponed as long as possible ; not because he was of that greedy and short-sighted class of bloodsuckers found at Monte Carlo and elsewhere who regard every new-comer with jealous hatred, as a possibly lucky player and a rival who may rob him of his substance—he was far too generous and philosophical to entertain such mean senti-ments—but simply because the existing state of things was so extremely pleasant that he did not wish to change it for any other.

Moreover, he had the true gambler's superstition about changing of luck ; and his luck might change in leaving Monte Carlo. For it was evident that if Harding was to play it must not be there. The season was now in full swing. Every day fresh crowds were pouring into the Casino. Harding might be recognised at his very first *séance*, and then any disaster might be possible.

' M—yes, old chappie,' said he reflectively.

'On the whole, I think it about the best thing we can do. A man can't play and mope at the same time. But we won't stay here. We've had enough of this place.'

'Yes; now there's no Liz about, the house is like a sepulchre. I never knew how much she was to us till she went away.'

Already he began to think he had behaved like a fool in that affair; he came in time to regard it as the silliest thing he had ever done in his life.

'And we won't play at Monte Carlo,' pursued the General with a sigh. 'There's such a herd of second-rate persons there, and they are so aggressive and so rude. It's like a tramcar; you have to fight for a seat, and when you've got it, you find you've a pick-pocket on one side and a woman who eats peppermint on the other.'

'Anywhere you like, only, for Heaven's sake, let's get out of this sharp.'

They left Mentone the next day, and journeyed right across France to Fontarabia, a gaming place in the North of Spain, quite out of the tourist's track, and known only to old hands like the General.

When the season ended at Fontarabia they went down to Saxon-les-Bains, and in the winter they came up to St. Sebastian, and thence in due course, with the rest of their tribe, they shifted their quarters to some other place where the excitement of play and fast living was to be found.

Habitual pleasure-seekers are the dullest people in the world ; but not one of them was so lumpish and heavy and sour as Harding. No one ever heard him laugh, or knew him to do a kind action for anybody ; and yet, not so very long ago the slightest thing would set him roaring with laughter, the smallest appeal to sympathy draw quick and generous response from him.

He had outlived sentiment, and saw everything from a hard, material point of view.
Why should he laugh who saw no fun in
anything ? Why should he feel for the mis-
fortunes of others who was getting callous
even to the sorrows of his own life ? There
were no lights and shadows in his sunless
existence, no contrast of hope and disappoint-
ment—all things seemed to his numbed
senses monotonous, same, and worthless.

He played as he drank—not for pleasure,
but relief and distraction, as some take
narcotics to cure insomnia, and with the
same result : the dose had to be continually
increased to produce the desired effect. And
as he would sit over his bottle, bibbing and
bibbing until his brain got muddled and
perverse, so he would play, staking his
money a handful at a time, recklessly in-
different whether he lost or won, while the
chances were fairly equal, scarcely knowing

what he did, until some persistent run of ill-luck would sting him and rouse a savage feeling of resentment ; then he would obstinately contend against some luckless series, or put all he had upon a number that had just turned up, the odds against him being about thirty-seven to one.

He found companions who stuck to him close enough while he kept his purse open, and left him the moment he drew the strings. There is no need to trace his history through those three years of debasement, of going down step by step from the rank of a gentleman to the level of a blackguard ; it is pleasant neither to write about nor to read about.

During this time the General's life was not altogether a happy one. In the first place, he seemed decidedly to have left his luck behind him at Monte Carlo. One after the other every system he tried broke down

before the relentless 'series.' His losses were
not great, to be sure, but his gains were
proportionately small. A constant player, if
he be prudent also, may fairly calculate upon
his loss at the end of the year being brought
by the invariable laws of chance to exactly
the two and a half per cent. exacted by the
bank upon the stakes ; and, as a matter of
fact, the General, who restricted his venture
to a modest two hundred and fifty francs a
day, lost no more than three hundred pounds
at the tables in those three years.

With an equal share of Harding's capital
at the beginning, he could have gone on
playing at this rate to a patriarchal age, and
lived in an enviable state of self-content. But
circumstances prevented Harding's fortune
being realized and divided all in one batch,
or he would have quitted his companion very
soon after they left Mentone, and he perceived what kind of a player he had for a

partner. It came in piecemeal, as one farm after another was disposed of, at ever-widening distances, and in such diminishing quantity that it became obvious there must soon be no more to divide.

A much larger fortune than his would have been inadequate to meet for many years such enormous drains as Harding put upon it by his reckless prodigality and foolhardy play. He was driving post-haste along the road to ruin ; the General knew it, perceived his utter inability to put on the brake or turn the driver's course, and, what was the worst part of it all for him, he was compelled to stick in the same trap.

Things were brought to a crisis in the spring of the third year, when a letter came from Playfair enclosing a cheque for five hundred pounds, the price of Sir Henry Harding's last acres, less legal expenses, and with it a polite intimation that the worthy solicitors felt it advisable to close accounts with their respected client.

A deeper shade of gloom fell upon Harding's face, as the reflection that now he had not a single stick of timber or inch of ground to call his own raised once more that old remorseful speculation on what might have been. But it passed away with another reflection as the garçon brought him his morning dose of absinthe.

'What's the good of race, or estate, or name, or anything, to such as I ?'

Later on, when he had changed the cheque, he divided the bundle of notes in two, and, shoving one half towards the General, he said :

'There's your half, old man ; now for the last flutter.'

'A flutter !' There was mockery in that word applied to such a log as he.

At the end of the evening's play the

General met Harding, and in a jubilant tone said :

' It's all right, dear old chappie ; the *boule de neige* has doubled my capital.'

' Good job,' replied Harding. ' I'm cleared out—every sou. I felt No. 26 wouldn't win, so I planked all I had on it and lost.'

A little more faith in his *boule de neige* would have induced the General to part company with Harding even now, and leave him to settle his account with Destiny and the Hôtel de Madrid as he might. But he was too old now, despite the illusions of his sixty and odd years, to be cheated by shadows, and there was substance yet to be got out of Harding by careful management.

He had not heard anything of Denise ; but he felt sure she had not parted with all that fifty thousand she had so prudently secured for herself out of the estate.

CHAPTER XXX.

THE BATTLE OF FLOWERS.

'I've not had a good week,' said the General one morning, 'not a memorably good week, dear boy, since we left Monte Carlo. Now there, you know, I always was lucky.'

'I don't know why the deuce you haven't thought of that before.'

'Well, we've never been so confoundedly pinched as we are at present. I think, old chappie, we ought to go there.'

'It's all the same to me. Go if you like. Only '—after a moment's pause—'I don't want to put up at the Villa Bella Vista again.'

' I only wish we had the means to do it, dear boy.'

The Villa Bella Vista, with its passion-flowers and roses, came back to Harding's memory; a paradise it seemed to him now, seen from the purgatory of moral debasement and conscious ignominy in which he existed. ' If I had it to do again,' he thought, ' I'd not be such a sentimental idiot. Liz might have made a decent fellow of me by this time. She did love me—pretty Liz!—no mistake about that.' And Liz, in her quaint Dutch bonnet and dove-coloured dress, rose another spectre to add to his self-reproach.

He flung his glass down on the pavement, shivering it to pieces, in childish, idiotic rage, because these recollections came unbidden to torment him. What was the use of being a log if he might not enjoy a log's insensibility? Why might not a man live like a cabbage till the time came for him to die and rot? Why

should these confounded thoughts crop up
again just because those last acres were gone?
Was it all to begin over again? Was no
rest to be got?

When they reached the Riviera the General
selected a grubby hotel on the outskirts of
Mentone for their residence, wishing to subject Harding to the physical discomforts of
poverty as a means of making him more
readily accept the proposal he should soon
have to submit.

'We are so deucedly hard up, dear boy,'
he said, 'that we shan't have a five-franc
piece to punt with if we don't economize.'

'Have it your own way,' said Harding, and
he put up with the dirty linen and greasy
cuisine, and third - class railway journeys
to Monte Carlo, patiently enough for a
week.

Then one morning, on their way to the
station, he stopped before an enormous

placard and read down the programme of
the carnival at Nice.

'What's to-day?' he asked.

'The fifth.'

'Battle of flowers on to-day.'

'I prefer roulette, old chappie.'

'I don't.   We'll have a trap, get a couple
of big noses and a basket of violets, and make
fools of ourselves.'

'It will cost a hundred francs.   Who's to
pay for it?'

'You.   What does it matter if it costs two
hundred?   You've got more than that.   Do
you begrudge it?' he asked, turning savagely
on the General.   'Whose money is it, after
all?'

'Dear boy, dear boy!' remonstrated the
General.   'We may forget that we are poor;
but we must not forget that we are gentlemen.'

One would have thought that he really was
a gentleman, and a fine one, too, by the air

he gave himself. When Harding was about to get into a third-class carriage, the General drew him away, and, opening the door of a first-class compartment, stood back, raising his hat, for him to enter first. It might be a farce, but the General was not one to clown his part.

At Nice they went to Laurent's, and found the choice of vehicles reduced to three. Harding insisted upon taking a small donkey-cart drawn by two donkeys in tandem, and ordered the equipage to be decorated with orange-blossom while they were lunching. Then he bought a couple of enormous noses, one for himself and the other for the General, and a child's cradle which he filled with violets. Heaven knows what motive he had for this folly; certainly it was not with any sense of humour, for he made these preparations as gloomily as though they were for a funeral. Possibly he saw that the whole affair was vulgar and in bad taste, and he went in for it with the same perversity that led him to stake his money madly at the tables.

The General would have made a stand against wearing that long nose and making himself part of the sorry exhibition ; but he had special reasons at this time for humouring his companion and bringing him into an indulgent humour, having come now to a very critical juncture, which involved nothing less than some sort of a confession of his own villainy.   He could not afford to stand on his dignity and oppose Harding, and the only hope was that a new caprice would seize his companion before the battle which would lead him to abandon the silly freak.

But Harding was in his sourest mood to-day, and stuck obstinately to his idea, the more so, maybe, because he saw it was against the General's inclinations.   He himself adjusted the old man's nose, on the end of which was an enormous bluebottle, before he put on his own.

'You look a regular beast, old man,' he said, with the grunt that was his nearest approach to a laugh. 'Pity it hides your venerable moustache.'

They got into the cart, Harding taking the driver's place, and the General sitting beside him on the narrow seat with the cradle of flowers wedged in between his long legs, which was very uncomfortable, besides being disgustingly grotesque.

Then they drove down the boulevard amidst the jeers of the masquers, and, entering the course, fell in with the procession of gaily ornamented equipages moving slowly along before the densely packed throng behind the barriers, the grand-stands, and the tribune. They were pelted with flowers, but Harding never returned a single bouquet

—he left that part of the tomfoolery to the General. He, with his head sunk in his shoulders, took no notice of anyone or anything but the donkeys he was driving.

'Don't you think we've had about enough of it, dear boy?' suggested the General, when they had gone twice round the course, and the cradle was emptied.

'No; mean to be the last on the course; get my money's worth out of these donkeys.'

And so he drove twice more up and down the course with dogged perseverance, looking neither to the right nor to the left, and began a third. At a little distance from the grandstand there was a block which compelled him to halt. Just as he was starting afresh, a child's shrill laugh, high and clear like a silver bell, struck on his ear, and for the first time he turned his heavy eyes from the backs of his donkeys and glanced at the crowd.

A gentleman was holding a child up to

look at the funny man with the donkeys.
The child screamed anew with laughter as
Harding turned his grotesque face, and, look-
ing down at a sweet little lady, cried:

'Look, mammie, look! Funny man! Di
me f'owers!'

The lady put a bunch of pansies from her
basket into the chubby little hand, and the
child tossed it towards Harding with another
shrill peal of laughter. The procession
moved on. Harding's whip-hand fell, the
whip was caught by the wheel and dragged
from his nerveless fingers unnoticed as he
strained round to catch a last glimpse of the
group. The child had found a fresh object
of delight, and the sweet little lady was giving
fresh flowers to throw to another.

They knew not who he was—that funny
man down whose cheek a single tear was
trickling; but he knew them. It was Bernard Thrale who held the child, and mammie

was Denise—his own wife, more beautiful than ever for the maternal tenderness in her face, sweet and smiling as if his ruin had cast no shadow on her life!

The General recognised them, and without surprise. At the beginning of the week he had telegraphed to Denise — a telegram, though it cost a trifle more than a letter, is cheap as avoiding the necessity of tedious explanation—addressing the wire to Harding Court, on the chance of its finding her there or being forwarded :

' Harry here.   Come at once, if you would save him.—Address, General G., chez Boulot, Café de Paris, Monte Carlo.'

That was his message ; and the promptitude with which Denise had responded to the appeal augured so well for the replenishment of his exhausted funds that the General had reason to feel well satisfied. He was not less pleased to mark the token of emotion upon Harding's cheek. Emotional persons, if you only know how to handle them, are so much more easily managed than those of the apathetic, calculating sort.

They were a long while reaching the exit, the course being now at its fullest; but as soon as they were outside Harding, without a word, flung down the reins, tore off his papier-maché nose, and, jumping down from the cart, pushed his way through the scattering crowd in the direction of the grand-stand. There was no definite purpose in his mind beyond the simple object of finding his wife, of feasting his eyes upon her beauty, of setting his heart bleeding anew with the cruel stabs of remorse. What he should do if he found her, what he should say if they spoke to him, he never for a moment considered.

It was not until the course was empty, the crowd dispersed—not until he had gone a dozen times from end to end of the thronged boulevard, glancing from face to face, examining each group, peering into the open restaurants, and finally abandoning the hopeless task from sheer exhaustion, that he began to speculate on the possible outcome of meeting Denise and Thrale.

He felt sure he must find them sooner or later. As soon as he was a bit set up he'd have another hunt. If they had gone home because of their child it didn't matter; he would search for them to-morrow. And when they met, what should he do? He knew. It didn't take long to decide that.

There was no thought of vengeance in his purpose; no reproach, recrimination or passionate appeal presented themselves to his imagination. There should be no 'scene,' no theatrical nonsense of any kind. He'd

shake hands with them if they would let him ;
bygones should be bygones ; he wouldn't
rake up past grievances or say anything to
make them uncomfortable, if only they would
treat him as a kind of old friend and allow
him to call and see them from time to time.
Anything in the world if he might only look
at Denise now and then—Denise who loved
him once, whom nothing could make him
cease to love.

A half-drowned cur, dragging its benumbed
limbs from the ooze had more courage than
this wretch, soddened to the very core of his
heart with misery.

CHAPTER XXXI.

NEMESIS.

HARDING slept at Nice that night—if such rest as he got might be called sleep—and began his search again next morning. Towards the evening, when hunger began to tell upon him, he found he had not enough to pay for a two-franc dinner. Without money he could not continue his search. But he knew where he should find the General, and, scraping his loose pieces together, he found enough to buy a third-class ticket to Monte Carlo.

On the steps of the Casino he met the General, looking less jaunty than usual—

indeed, the old man's position was so gravely embarrassing that it needed extraordinary assurance to conceal his anxiety. At the sight of Harding he brightened up wonderfully.

'Dear boy, you are the very Johnnie I was hoping to find!' said he, grasping Harding's limp hand.

'Same to you,' replied Harry sullenly. 'I want a hundred francs.'

'So do I, dear chappie. Fifty, twenty, five —anything you can let me have, for I'm absolutely stone-broke. The most extraordinary down-run on red I ever knew; twelve consecutive reds, and the eleventh cleared me out completely. Where are you going, dear boy?' as Harding, with a grunt, tore his arm from the General's amicable grasp and turned on his heel.

'Back to Nice.'

'Mentone's nearer; and we can get lodging there on credit.'

'I'm going to Nice, I tell you,' Harding replied, striding westward.

'Tell me why, dear boy,' the General asked, with difficulty keeping pace and speaking at the same time.

'To look for *them.*'

'If you mean Mr. Thrale and your wife, you'll not find them there. They're at Mentone.'

'At Mentone?'

Harding stopped dead short as he put the question.

'At Mentone. Met them on the platform when I got out of the train night before last. I'll tell you all about it if you'll go a bit slower.'

Harding was striding off now eastward.

'Out with it,' he said, slackening his pace.

'They were only in Nice for a few hours. It was the first break on their journey from——'

'How do you know?' asked Harding, again stopping short.

'They told me.'

'You have spoken to her, and she to you?' cried the poor wretch, in astonishment and envy.

'Of course; why not?'

'Lucky beggar! lucky beggar! Come on. Do you know where they're staying?'

'To be sure.'

The General pulled out his note-case and found a slip of paper. Another stop as Harding took the slip and read it by the light of a gas-lamp.

'Why, it's her writing!' said he, with a foolish titter. 'Her writing—her own hand!'

He clasped the piece of paper between his palms; looked at it again; lifted it and pressed it hard against his flabby cheek.

The General cleared his throat. It was a ticklish thing, this, he had to reveal.

'I've never told you my history, dear boy,' he began, as they moved on.

'Damn your history!' he exclaimed; and then 'Hôtel d'Angleterre' he murmured, as if to print it upon his memory.

'I think it's my duty, you know, to tell you something about my past.'

'Fire away, if you like.' He held the paper up in the moonlight. 'I can read it by the moon,' he said, sniggering. ' " Denise Harding." She still keeps my name,' he added, with a semblance of pride in his tone.

'Of course.'

'I thought she would have taken Thrale's.'

'Well, as I was saying, you know, dear boy, about two-and-twenty years ago——'

'Old man,' said Harding, in a timid voice, 'do you think she would speak to me?'

'Well, that depends on circumstances.'

'Oh, I promise I won't make a fool of myself—no fear! Not a word about the

past. No unpleasing allusions to their relations, you know. I've made up my mind
about that. I won't offend them—not for
the world! I just want them to regard me
as an acquaint—a sort of friend,' he urged
in an insinuating tone, fingering his ragged
beard apprehensively. 'If they would just
let me call upon them now and then—say,
once a week at the outside—to chat about
ordinary trifles with her—Denise !'

'I dare say that can be managed.'

'Oh, if you only could, old man! It'd
make such a lot of difference to me. I should
be so jolly grateful to you !'

He took the General's arm and pressed it,
the thumb and finger of the other hand in
his waistcoat-pocket softly smoothing the
slip of paper with her name on it.

They walked some little distance in silence,
Harding nursing his delightful project, the
General taxing his ingenuity to turn Hard-

ing's suggestion to account without commit-
ting himself.

But no; he could find no means of getting
money and escaping revelation at the same
time.   So he cleared his throat again, and
began his history once more.   He spun out
the details at considerable length, to gain
time for reflection and smooth the way.
That made no difference to Harding; he
pursued his own delightful train of thought,
as oblivious of the General's history as of the
lap of the waves amongst the rocks below.

So in this manner they walked along the
beautiful Corniche Road, now in full moonlight, now in deep shade, as the path followed the sinuous contour of the precipitous
mountain-side, until Harding's ear caught
a word that bore connection with the recollections revolving in his brain.

'What's that you said about Victoria?' he
asked.

'I was saying that, for reasons which it is unnecessary to particularize, I left Mrs. Gordon in the second year of our marriage at Victoria, and took my passage to Marseilles. There the happy thought occurred to me to run down to Monte Carlo and try my hand at the tables——'

'Only the eternal Monte Carlo!' thought Harding; and then he said to himself that he would certainly get his hair cut and his beard shaved off—or trimmed would be better, perhaps, as his face had got so ugly—before he ventured to call upon Denise. They walked best part of another mile before his meditations were again broken; then, stopping, he said:

'Hold hard! I didn't catch that about Denise; go back a bit.'

'On the top of the stairs, just against my door on the landing—you remember my diggings in Piccadilly?'

'Yes, yes.   Go on.'

'I kick my foot against something, strike
a vesta, and there, to my complete bewilder-
ment, I find a pretty little girl, about seventeen, sitting on the top of an old trunk, her
shoulders resting in the angles of the wall,
and sound asleep.   I tap her on the shoulder,
and, as she rouses a bit, "My dear young
woman," says I, "who are you, and what on
earth are you doing here?"   "Oh, if you
please," says she, rubbing her eyes, "I am
Denise, and I've just come from Australia,
and want to see General Gordon."   "Well,
my dear," says I, "*I* am General Gordon."
"Then you're my father!" says she.'

'What!' cried Harding, shifting his position to confront him.   'This girl you are
speaking of was Denise—my wife?'

'Yes, and my daughter.'

'Your daughter?'

The General shrugged his shoulders.

'So I am told,' said he.

'Wait ; I must understand this. Sit down here.'

They were upon a bridge that crossed a ravine. Far below the breaking waves flashed in the moonlight like electric sparks. The General did not like the look of it, and would have gone on, with some excuse about his susceptibility to rheumatism and the coldness of the seat ; but Harding was too excited to listen to such trifles, and forced the old man to sit down, turning sideways to face each other.

'Now go on,' he said.

'Well,' continued the General, with as much ease as he could assume—'well, dear boy, what was I to do ? I should have liked to do the right thing, of course, especially as Denise was a girl any man might be proud to own as his daughter. But my circumstances would not permit it. The want of money

has been the ruin of my character. If I
had only had the settled income of, say, a
bishop——'

'Never mind your damned philosophy;
get on!'

'How could I do it, dear chappie? I had
barely enough to keep myself in that Piccadilly garret and pay my tailor's bill. I
couldn't afford to keep a house and servants,
furnish her with clothes and luxuries, and all
that. Besides, it didn't at all agree with my
tastes and habits. It wasn't to be done. I
put it to Denise plainly : " My dear," says I,
" you may be my daughter for all I know to
the contrary, but I can't afford to own it.
You must earn your living as a domestic
drudge. You must go back to Victoria,
or you must agree to my planting you on
some wealthy family of my acquaintance as
the destitute daughter of an old friend."
After some little consideration, she accepted

the latter alternative, and I planted her on Mrs. Balfour.'

'Then, it was you who first taught her to deceive.'

'I admit the justice of that reproach, dear chappie, for had I not taught her to deceive, you would never have met her, and you might have been a happier man.'

'Oh, I don't reproach you—not I! It's not my love for her nor my wasted life that I regret. If it were to do again, I'd do it, though I lost her again. Just to touch her hand once more would pay for all.'

'That's sound philosophy, dear boy. What does it matter how much we lost yesterday if we win to-day?'

'If——'

'It's never too late to win.'

'Don't talk such rot to me; I'm past dreaming.'

' But not past awaking, dear boy.'

'What do you mean ?'

'Supposing—remember, I'm a dreamer, dear chappie,' said the General tentatively, parenthetically edging himself a little further from Harding and the dangerous side of the parapet—'supposing you should awake to-night to find you had been dreaming three years ?'

He paused, but Harding made no response. His back was directly against the full moon ; the General could not discern a feature of his face, still less the spasmodic twitching of his lips, the gathering frenzy in his eye, and he continued :

'Supposing I could show you that every wrong you have been brooding over was simply imaginary ?'

He paused again, inwardly cursing the moonlight that prevented him seeing the effect of his revelation, doubting if it

had yet touched Harding's sluggish understanding.

'Supposing,' he pursued, 'that I could
prove to you that Denise is yet a faithful
wife, Thrale still a true and loyal friend—
what would you say to me?'

'Say to you!' cried Harding, springing
up. 'Say! Why, I'd fall upon my knees
and bless you as an angel come to snatch me
from damnation!'

'And on the principle advanced just now,
when you would have forgiven Denise all
for the sake of touching her hand, you would
bear me no ill will for any little irregularities
of which I may have been guilty in these past
three years?'

'There's not a thing I couldn't forgive for
such a joy!'

'Then,' continued the General rapidly,
encouraged by success, 'then, to crown your
joy, if I could show not only that your wife

is pure, your friend unchanged, but also that
the child who cried to you at Nice was your
own son——'

With the fury of a madman, and with a
madman's inconsistency, Harding sprang
upon the General, and, clutching him by
the throat, cried :

'Tell me this is true, or I'll strangle
you !'

The General struggled to free himself.
His hat fell, striking the parapet, and
toppling over into the abyss.

'You're choking me—are you mad?' he
gasped.

'I shall be, if this hope you've raised is
false.   Tell me it's true!' cried Harding
fiercely.

'By God, it's true—every word of it !'

'And the man I saw in my wife's room ?'

'It was I—I swear it !'

Harding was silent, but his fingers tight-

ened on the old man's throat, and, holding
him at arm's length, he shook him, looking
into his distorted face with relentless
vengeance. It took his brain, excited to
the pitch of madness, but a little while to
realize the whole truth.

'And you knew this from the beginning?'
he muttered. 'You have known it these
four years, and seen me sinking day by day
without remorse or pity—sinking deep into
a hell beyond redemption — sinking from
manhood to beasthood, to such a vile condition that I dare not claim wife or friend or
child for mine!'

'Let me go—let me go!' gasped the
General.

'Oh, you shall go soon enough!' cried
Harding.

He suffered the old man to slip down upon
the road ; then, gripping him about the waist,
he lifted him up as if he had been a bag of

shavings, and threw him on the parapet, face downwards.

'That's where you are going,' he said, holding the helpless wretch's head down by the nape of the neck over the chasm. 'Down there, where the water shines amongst the rocks.' He thrust the old head further forward, while the General clutched at the parapet, tearing the finger-nails from his fingers in his frantic efforts to escape. 'I'll give you time to pray—not to me, for you've left no mercy in my soul. Pray to Heaven to forgive you for robbing me of wife and child and friend, of honour and name, and all hope of salvation.'

The General screamed for help, feeling his fingers breaking and his body slowly sliding forward under the steady thrust upon his neck.

'Go; I've no more time to waste on you,' said Harding, spluttering through the inky blood that now welled up into his mouth at every breath. 'You shall be first down there—go !'

The old man screamed again as his fingers broke away from the parapet and he felt his balance go ; then headlong he shot down through space. He struck the sharp rocks with a dull thud, but there was no sound after that save the gentle lapping of the waves.

CHAPTER XXXII.

THE END.

HARDING felt dizzy and sick and faint, not with the reflection that he had killed a man with whom he had lived in a kind of brotherhood for three years, or with apprehension of the consequences to himself when the murder was discovered : for his sole thought was of finding Denise, of showing her how he had been deceived, of justifying himself, of claiming her forgiveness for the base suspicion that had driven him to despair and ruin.

The cause was chiefly physical. He had been tramping about all day without food, and on the top of that there was this other affair. It was evident he had ruptured a vessel again, not seriously, as on the previous occasion, or it would have floored him at once as it had then. He would be all right again presently ; so he sat down on the parapet for two minutes, wiping the sweat from his clammy temples and trying to persuade himself that the hæmorrhage was abating.

Then the thought that he had an hour's walk before him, and that the Hôtel d'Angleterre might be closed when he reached Mentone, gave him energy, if not strength, and he started up with the dogged determination not to succumb under this attack. The road seemed to give under his feet, the rocks to be going up and up before him ; he had to fix his eyes upon a distant mark to make a straight line, just as if he had been drinking heavily. As he staggered on, a man came into sight and stopped in his path, asking if it were he who had screamed aloud just now. Harding waved him aside with his arm, and would have passed ; but the man, seeing blood upon his beard, caught him by the shoulder, and only just in time, for Harding, spinning round on one heel, fell fainting into his arms.

When he recovered consciousness the glare of a paraffin lamp was in his eyes, and the light falling on a buffet, with many bottles and an urn for the garçon's *pourboires*, showed him that he was in a café. For a moment he could not understand how he had come there, nor why he lay at full length on this mattress, with a billiard-board, of all things in the world, for a bedstead ; then it flashed upon him that he was to find Denise and tell her all, and he struggled to rise.

A hand was laid upon his shoulder gently, but he had no strength to combat even the

lightest touch, and, falling back, he found a
motherly woman in a marmotte leaning over
him.

'Mentone—Mentone!' he said in desperation.

'You must not move, sir,' answered the
woman in French loudly, as the invalid was
clearly a foreigner.   'See, you've made yourself bad again.   Here's a soft clean serviette.
There, lie so.   My husband's gone over to
Cabé Roquebrun for the doctor.'

'Mentone,' murmured Harding feebly.

'Yes; you shall go to Mentone to-
morrow.'

'No more!' thought Harding.   'It's all
up with me.   I shan't see Mentone again;'
and a vision of the garden and its flowers,
of the blue sea and sky framed in twining
roses and passion-flowers, came before his
closed eyes.   'Denise shall know I was all
right, then—that there was nothing wrong

between me and Liz. If I don't tell 'em, she and Bernard will think I ran away to live there with her. Oh, they mustn't think so badly of me as that !'

And with that fear he endeavoured to raise his hand and get the paper from his waist-coat-pocket, but his hand was like lead and his muscles seemed fibreless. The woman understood what he wanted to do, and, feeling in his waistcoat - pocket, brought out the slip of paper and read it at his mute bidding.

' To-morrow,' she said, having read the address and comprehended his wish.

' Now, now,' he muttered.

She pointed to the clock, and explained the impossibility of sending to Mentone at this hour, of awaking the people of the hotel, and of finding any vehicle to bring a lady across. ' To-morrow,' she repeated sooth-ingly, ' to-morrow.'

'Too late,' thought he; 'I shall be dead when they come. They will see only the wreck of what was once a decent man. They'll learn that I have lived four years in debauchery, but they'll never know the truth. They'll say, "It's a mercy he is gone; we couldn't have won him back; he would always have been a trouble to us—a shame to his child." Oh, if they only knew the misery of these years, my yearning to bring back the past.' Then he began to cry in sheer pity of himself.

He lapsed into unconsciousness of surrounding things as the life slowly ebbed away, and passed the night in a long dream made up of memories chiefly of happy days. But towards the end his perceptive faculties revived, and his feelings had a manlier and healthier tone, as if invigorated by those dreams of his better life. He thought now, not of his own past misery and suffering, but of his wife's, and the tears that ran down his cheek were no longer for himself.

A mist was gathering over him, so that he could see nothing clearly, when he felt his hand lifted up and pressed, warm breath upon his brow and gentle lips upon his eyes.

'Who—who?' he asked faintly, yet with joy.

'Dear Harry, it is I—your wife——'

'Poor wife, poor wife! Dear love! Is that Bernard?'

'Yes, here I am, old chap.'

'Take my other hand. There! Friend and wife — once more mine. Think of me, not as I am, but as I should have been.'

'Here's our son, dear. Your boy, Harry.'

'Harry—my boy! This little thing his hand! May he be strong and brave—and have faith—faith—faith in others more than in himself.   Harry, be good — good to mammie.'

And then, that they might not see his agony, he turned his face aside, knowing that the end was come.

THE END.

BILLING AND SONS, PRINTERS, GUILDFORD.

LIST OF BOOKS PUBLISHED BY

CHATTO & WINDUS

214 PICCADILLY, LONDON, W.

About (Edmond).—The Fellah: An Egyptian Novel. Translated by
Sir RANDAL ROBERTS. Post 8vo, illustrated boards, 2s.

Adams (W. Davenport), Works by.
A Dictionary of the Drama: being a comprehensive Guide to the Plays, Playwrights, Players,
and Playhouses of the United Kingdom and America, from the Earliest Times to the Present
Day. Crown 8vo, half-bound, 12s. 6d. [*Preparing.*
Quips and Quiddities. Selected by W. DAVENPORT ADAMS. Post 8vo, cloth limp, 2s. 6d.

Agony Column (The) of 'The Times,' from 1800 to 1870. Edited,
with an Introduction, by ALICE CLAY. Post 8vo, cloth limp, 2s. 6d.

Aïdé (Hamilton), Novels by. Post 8vo, illustrated boards, 2s. each.
Carr of Carrlyon. | **Confidences.**

Albert (Mary).—Brooke Finchley's Daughter. Post 8vo, picture
boards, 2s.; cloth limp, 2s. 6d.

Alden (W. L.).—A Lost Soul: Being the Confession and Defence of
Charles Lindsay. Fcap. 8vo, cloth boards, 1s. 6d.

Alexander (Mrs.), Novels by. Post 8vo, illustrated boards, 2s. each.
Maid, Wife, or Widow? | **Valerie's Fate.**

Allen (F. M.).—Green as Grass. With a Frontispiece. Crown 8vo,
cloth, 3s. 6d.

Allen (Grant), Works by.
The Evolutionist at Large. Crown 8vo, cloth extra, 6s.
Post-Prandial Philosophy. Crown 8vo, art linen, 3s. 6d.
Moorland Idylls. Crown 8vo, cloth decorated, 6s.

Crown 8vo, cloth extra, 3s. 6d. each; post 8vo, illustrated boards, 2s. each.

Philistia.	**In all Shades.**	**Dumaresq's Daughter.**
Babylon. 12 Illustrations.	**The Devil's Die.**	**The Duchess of Powysland**
Strange Stories. Frontis.	**This Mortal Coil.**	**Blood Royal.**
The Beckoning Hand.	**The Tents of Shem.** Frontis.	**Ivan Greet's Masterpiece.**
For Maimie's Sake.	**The Great Taboo.**	**The Scallywag.** 24 Illusts.

Crown 8vo, cloth extra, 3s. 6d. each.

At Market Value. | **Under Sealed Orders.**

Dr. Palliser's Patient. Fcap. 8vo, cloth boards, 1s. 6d.

Anderson (Mary).—Othello's Occupation: A Novel. Crown 8vo,
cloth, 3s. 6d.

Arnold (Edwin Lester), Stories by.
The Wonderful Adventures of Phra the Phœnician. Crown 8vo, cloth extra, with 12
Illustrations by H. M. PAGET, 3s. 6d.; post 8vo, illustrated boards, 2s.
The Constable of St. Nicholas. With Frontispiece by S. L. WOOD. Crown 8vo, cloth, 3s. 6d.

Artemus Ward's Works. With Portrait and Facsimile. Crown 8vo,
cloth extra, 7s. 6d.—Also a POPULAR EDITION, post 8vo, picture boards, 2s.
The Genial Showman: The Life and Adventures of ARTEMUS WARD. By EDWARD P.
HINGSTON. With a Frontispiece. Crown 8vo, cloth extra, 3s. 6d.

Ashton (John), Works by. Crown 8vo, cloth extra, 7s. 6d. each.
History of the Chap-Books of the 18th Century. With 334 Illustrations.
Social Life in the Reign of Queen Anne. With 85 Illustrations.
Humour, Wit, and Satire of the Seventeenth Century. With 82 Illustrations.
English Caricature and Satire on Napoleon the First. With 115 Illustrations.
Modern Street Ballads. With 57 Illustrations.

Bacteria, Yeast Fungi, and Allied Species, A Synopsis of. By
W. B. GROVE, B.A. With 87 Illustrations. Crown 8vo, cloth extra, 3s. 6d.

Bardsley (Rev. C. Wareing, M.A.), Works by.
English Surnames: Their Sources and Significations. Crown 8vo, cloth, 7s. 6d.
Curiosities of Puritan Nomenclature. Crown 8vo, cloth extra, 6s.

Baring Gould (Sabine, Author of 'John Herring,' &c.), Novels by.
Crown 8vo, cloth extra, 3s. 6d. each; post 8vo, illustrated boards, 2s. each.
Red Spider. | Eve.

Barr (Robert: Luke Sharp), Stories by. Cr. 8vo, cl., 3s. 6d. each.
In a Steamer Chair. With Frontispiece and Vignette by DEMAIN HAMMOND.
From Whose Bourne, &c. With 47 Illustrations by HAL HURST and others.

A Woman Intervenes. With 8 Illustrations by HAL HURST. Crown 8vo, cloth extra, 6s.
Revenge! With numerous Illustrations. Crown 8vo, cloth extra, 6s.　　　　[Shortly.

Barrett (Frank), Novels by.
Post 8vo, illustrated boards, 2s. each; cloth, 2s. 6d. each.

Fettered for Life.	A Prodigal's Progress.
The Sin of Olga Zassoulich.	John Ford; and His Helpmate.
Between Life and Death.	A Recoiling Vengeance.
Folly Morrison. | Honest Davie.	Lieut. Barnabas. | Found Guilty.
Little Lady Linton.	For Love and Honour.

The Woman of the Iron Bracelets. Cr. 8vo, cloth, 3s. 6d.; post 8vo, boards, 2s.; cl.limp, 2s. 6d.
The Harding Scandal. 2 vols., 10s. net.　　　　[Shortly.

Barrett (Joan).—Monte Carlo Stories. Fcap. 8vo, cloth, 1s. 6d.

Beaconsfield, Lord. By T. P. O'CONNOR, M.P. Cr. 8vo, cloth, 5s.

Beauchamp (Shelsley).—Grantley Grange. Post 8vo, boards, 2s.

Beautiful Pictures by British Artists: A Gathering of Favourites
from the Picture Galleries, engraved on Steel. Imperial 4to, cloth extra, gilt edges, 21s.

Besant (Sir Walter) and James Rice, Novels by.
Crown 8vo, cloth extra, 3s. 6d. each; post 8vo, illustrated boards, 2s. each; cloth limp, 2s. 6d. each.

Ready-Money Mortiboy.	By Celia's Arbour.
My Little Girl.	The Chaplain of the Fleet.
With Harp and Crown.	The Seamy Side.
This Son of Vulcan.	The Case of Mr. Lucraft, &c.
The Golden Butterfly.	'Twas in Trafalgar's Bay, &c.
The Monks of Thelema.	The Ten Years' Tenant, &c.

∗ There is also a LIBRARY EDITION of the above Twelve Volumes, handsomely set in new type on a
large crown 8vo page, and bound in cloth extra, 6s. each; and a POPULAR EDITION of The Golden
Butterfly, medium 8vo, 6d.; cloth, 1s.—NEW EDITIONS, printed in large type on crown 8vo laid paper,
bound in figured cloth, 3s. 6d. each, are also in course of publication.

Besant (Sir Walter), Novels by.
Crown 8vo, cloth extra, 3s. 6d. each; post 8vo, illustrated boards, 2s. each; cloth limp, 2s. 6d. each.
All Sorts and Conditions of Men. With 12 Illustrations by FRED. BARNARD
The Captains' Room, &c. With Frontispiece by E. J. WHEELER.
All in a Garden Fair. With 6 Illustrations by HARRY FURNISS.
Dorothy Forster. With Frontispiece by CHARLES GREEN.
Uncle Jack, and other Stories. | Children of Gibeon.
The World Went Very Well Then. With 12 Illustrations by A. FORESTIER.
Herr Paulus: His Rise, his Greatness, and his Fall. | The Bell of St. Paul's.
For Faith and Freedom. With Illustrations by A. FORESTIER and F. WADDY.
To Call Her Mine, &c. With 9 Illustrations by A. FORESTIER.
The Holy Rose, &c. With Frontispiece by F. BARNARD.
Armorel of Lyonesse: A Romance of To-day. With 12 Illustrations by F. BARNARD.
St. Katherine's by the Tower. With 12 Illustrations by C. GREEN.
Verbena Camellia Stephanotis, &c. With a Frontispiece by GORDON BROWNE.
The Ivory Gate. | The Rebel Queen.

Beyond the Dreams of Avarice. With 12 Illusts. by W. H. HYDE. Crown 8vo, cloth extra, 3s. 6d.
In Deacon's Orders, &c. With Frontispiece by A. FORESTIER. Crown 8vo, cloth, 6s.
The Master Craftsman. 2 vols., crown 8vo, 10s. net.　　　　[May

Fifty Years Ago. With 144 Plates and Woodcuts. Crown 8vo, cloth extra, 5s.
The Eulogy of Richard Jefferies. With Portrait. Crown 8vo, cloth extra, 6s.
London. With 125 Illustrations. Demy 8vo, cloth extra, 7s. 6d.
Westminster. With Etched Frontispiece by F. S. WALKER, R.P.E., and 130 Illustrations by
WILLIAM PATTEN and others. Demy 8vo, cloth, 18s.
Sir Richard Whittington. With Frontispiece. Crown 8vo, art linen, 3s. 6d.
Gaspard de Coligny. With a Portrait. Crown 8vo, art linen, 3s. 6d.
As we Are: As we May Be: Social Essays. Crown 8vo, linen, 6s.　　　　[Shortly.

Bechstein (Ludwig).—As Pretty as Seven, and other German
Stories. With Additional Tales by the Brothers GRIMM, and 98 Illustrations by RICHTER. Square
8vo, cloth extra, 6s. 6d.; gilt edges, 7s. 6d.

Beerbohm (Julius).—Wanderings in Patagonia; or, Life among
the Ostrich-Hunters. With Illustrations. Crown 8vo, cloth extra, 3s. 6d.

Bellew (Frank).—The Art of Amusing: A Collection of Graceful
Arts, Games, Tricks, Puzzles, and Charades. With 300 Illustrations. Crown 8vo, cloth extra, 4s. 6d.

Bennett (W. C., LL.D.).—Songs for Sailors. Post 8vo, cl. limp, 2s,

Bewick (Thomas) and his Pupils. By AUSTIN DOBSON. With 95
Illustrations. Square 8vo, cloth extra, 6s.

Bierce (Ambrose).—In the Midst of Life: Tales of Soldiers and
Civilians. Crown 8vo, cloth extra, 6s.; post 8vo, illustrated boards, 2s.

Bill Nye's History of the United States. With 146 Illustrations
by F. OPPER. Crown 8vo, cloth extra, 3s. 6d.

Bire (Edmond).—Diary of a Citizen of Paris during 'The
Terror.' Translated and Edited by JOHN DE VILLIERS. With 2 Photogravures. Two Vols., 8vo, cloth,
21s. [Shortly.

Blackburn's (Henry) Art Handbooks.

Academy Notes, 1875, 1877-86, 1889, 1890, 1892-1895, Illustrated, each 1s.
Academy Notes, 1896. 1s. [May.
Academy Notes, 1875-79. Complete in One Vol., with 600 Illustrations. Cloth, 6s.
Academy Notes, 1880-84. Complete in One Vol., with 700 Illustrations. Cloth, 6s.
Academy Notes, 1890-94. Complete in One Vol., with 800 Illustrations. Cloth, 7s. 6d.
Grosvenor Notes, 1877. 6d.
Grosvenor Notes, separate years from 1878-1890, each 1s.
Grosvenor Notes, Vol. I., 1877-82. With 300 Illustrations. Demy 8vo, cloth, 6s.
The Paris Salon, 1895. With 300 Facsimile Sketches. 3s.

Grosvenor Notes, Vol. II., 1883-87. With 300 Illustrations. Demy 8vo, cloth, 6s.
Grosvenor Notes, Vol. III., 1888-90. With 230 Illustrations. Demy 8vo cloth, 3s. 6d.
The New Gallery, 1888-1895. With numerous Illustrations, each 1s.
The New Gallery, 1896. [May.
The New Gallery, Vol. I., 1888-1892. With 250 Illustrations. Demy 8vo, cloth, 6s.
English Pictures at the National Gallery. With 114 Illustrations. 1s.
Old Masters at the National Gallery. With 128 Illustrations. 1s. 6d.
Illustrated Catalogue to the National Gallery. With 242 Illusts. Demy 8vo, cloth, 3s.

Blind (Mathilde), Poems by.
The Ascent of Man. Crown 8vo, cloth, 5s.
Dramas in Miniature. With a Frontispiece by F. MADOX BROWN. Crown 8vo, cloth, 5s.
Songs and Sonnets. Fcap. 8vo, vellum and gold, 5s.
Birds of Passage: Songs of the Orient and Occident. Second Edition. Crown 8vo, linen, 6s. net.

Bourget (Paul).—A Living Lie. Translated by JOHN DE VILLIERS.
With special Preface for the English Edition. Crown 8vo, cloth, 3s. 6d.

Bourne (H. R. Fox), Books by.
English Merchants: Memoirs in Illustration of the Progress of British Commerce. With numerous Illustrations. Crown 8vo, cloth extra, 7s. 6d.
English Newspapers: Chapters in the History of Journalism. Two Vols., demy 8vo, cloth, 25s.
The Other Side of the Emin Pasha Relief Expedition. Crown 8vo, cloth, 6s.

Bowers (George).—Leaves from a Hunting Journal. Coloured
Plates. Oblong folio, half-bound, 21s.

Boyle (Frederick), Works by. Post 8vo, illustrated bds., 2s. each.
Chronicles of No-Man's Land. | Camp Notes. | Savage Life.

Brand (John).—Observations on Popular Antiquities; chiefly
illustrating the Origin of our Vulgar Customs, Ceremonies, and Superstitions. With the Additions of Sir
HENRY ELLIS, and numerous Illustrations. Crown 8vo, cloth extra, 7s. 6d.

Brewer (Rev. Dr.), Works by.
The Reader's Handbook of Allusions, References, Plots, and Stories. Seventeenth Thousand. Crown 8vo, cloth extra, 7s. 6d.
Authors and their Works, with the Dates: Being the Appendices to 'The Reader's Handbook,' separately printed. Crown 8vo, cloth limp, 2s.
A Dictionary of Miracles. Crown 8vo, cloth extra, 7s. 6d.

Brewster (Sir David), Works by. Post 8vo, cloth, 4s. 6d. each.
More Worlds than One: Creed of the Philosopher and Hope of the Christian. With Plates.
The Martyrs of Science: GALILEO, TYCHO BRAHE, and KEPLER. With Portraits.
Letters on Natural Magic. With numerous Illustrations.

Brillat-Savarin.—Gastronomy as a Fine Art. Translated by
R. E. ANDERSON, M.A. Post 8vo, half-bound, 2s.

Brydges (Harold).—Uncle Sam at Home. With 91 Illustrations.
Post 8vo, illustrated boards, 2s.; cloth limp, 2s. 6d.

Buchanan (Robert), Novels, &c., by.
Crown 8vo, cloth extra, 3s. 6d. each; pos 8vo, illustrated boards, 2s. each.

The Shadow of the Sword.
A Child of Nature. With Frontispiece.
God and the Man. With 11 Illustrations by FRED. BARNARD.
The Martyrdom of Madeline. With Frontispiece by A. W. COOPER.

Love Me for Ever. With Frontispiece.
Annan Water. | Foxglove Manor.
The New Abelard.
Matt: A Story of a Caravan. With Frontispiece.
The Master of the Mine. With Frontispiece.
The Heir of Linne. | Woman and the Man.

Crown 8vo, cloth extra, 3s. 6d. each.
Red and White Heather. | Rachel Dene.

Lady Kilpatrick. Crown 8vo, cloth extra, 6s.
The Wandering Jew: a Christmas Carol. Crown 8vo, cloth, 6s,

The Charlatan. By ROBERT BUCHANAN and HENRY MURRAY. With a Frontispiece by T. H. ROBINSON. Crown 8vo, cloth, 3s. 6d.

Burton (Richard F.).—The Book of the Sword. With over 400 Illustrations. Demy 4to, cloth extra, 32s.

Burton (Robert).—The Anatomy of Melancholy. With Translations of the Quotations. Demy 8vo, cloth extra, 7s. 6d.
Melancholy Anatomised: An Abridgment of BURTON'S ANATOMY. Post 8vo, half-bd., 2s. 6d.

Caine (T. Hall), Novels by. Crown 8vo, cloth extra, 3s. 6d. each.; post 8vo, illustrated boards, 2s. each; cloth limp, 2s. 6d. each.
The Shadow of a Crime. | A Son of Hagar. | The Deemster.
A LIBRARY EDITION of The Deemster is now ready; and one of The Shadow of a Crime is in preparation, set in new type, crown 8vo, cloth decorated, 6s. each.

Cameron (Commander V. Lovett).—The Cruise of the 'Black Prince' Privateer. Post 8vo, picture boards, 2s.

Cameron (Mrs. H. Lovett), Novels by. Post 8vo, illust. bds. 2s. ea.
Juliet's Guardian. | Deceivers Ever.

Carlyle (Jane Welsh), Life of. By Mrs. ALEXANDER IRELAND. With Portrait and Facsimile Letter. Small demy 8vo, cloth extra, 7s. 6d.

Carlyle (Thomas).—On the Choice of Books. Post 8vo, cl., 1s. 6d.
Correspondence of Thomas Carlyle and R. W. Emerson, 1834-1872. Edited by C. E. NORTON. With Portraits. Two Vols., crown 8vo, cloth, 24s.

Carruth (Hayden).—The Adventures of Jones. With 17 Illustrations. Fcap. 8vo, cloth, 2s.

Chambers (Robert W.), Stories of Paris Life by. Long fcap. 8vo, cloth, 2s. 6d. each.
The King in Yellow. | In the Quarter.

Chapman's (George), Works. Vol. I., Plays Complete, including the Doubtful Ones.—Vol. II., Poems and Minor Translations, with Essay by A. C. SWINBURNE.—Vol. III., Translations of the Iliad and Odyssey. Three Vols., crown 8vo, cloth, 6s. each.

Chapple (J. Mitchell).—The Minor Chord: The Story of a Prima Donna. Crown 8vo, cloth, 3s. 6d.

Chatto (W. A.) and J. Jackson.—A Treatise on Wood Engraving, Historical and Practical. With Chapter by H. G. BOHN, and 450 fine Illusts. Large 4to, half-leather, 28s.

Chaucer for Children: A Golden Key. By Mrs. H. R. HAWEIS. With 8 Coloured Plates and 30 Woodcuts. Crown 4to, cloth extra, 3s. 6d.
Chaucer for Schools. By Mrs. H. R. HAWEIS. Demy 8vo, cloth limp, 2s. 6d.

Chess, The Laws and Practice of. With an Analysis of the Openings. By HOWARD STAUNTON. Edited by R. B. WORMALD. Crown 8vo, cloth, 5s.
The Minor Tactics of Chess: A Treatise on the Deployment of the Forces in obedience to Strategic Principle. By F. K. YOUNG and E. C. HOWELL. Long fcap. 8vo, cloth, 2s. 6d.
The Hastings Chess Tournament Book (Aug.-Sept., 1895). Containing the Official Report of the 231 Games played in the Tournament, with Notes by the Players, and Diagrams of Interesting Positions; Portraits and Biographical Sketches of the Chess Masters; and an Account of the Congress and its surroundings. Crown 8vo, cloth extra, 7s. 6d. net. [Shortly.

Clare (Austin).—For the Love of a Lass. Post 8vo, 2s.; cl., 2s. 6d.

Clive (Mrs. Archer), Novels by. Post 8vo, illust. boards, 2s. each.
Paul Ferroll. | Why Paul Ferroll Killed his Wife.

Clodd (Edward, F.R.A.S.).—Myths and Dreams. Cr. 8vo, 3s. 6d.

Cobban (J. Maclaren), Novels by.
The Cure of Souls. Post 8vo, Illustrated boards, 2s.
The Red Sultan. Crown 8vo, cloth extra, 3s. 6d. ; post 8vo, illustrated boards, 2s.
The Burden of Isabel. Crown 8vo, cloth extra, 3s. 6d.

Coleman (John).—Players and Playwrights I have Known. Two
Vols., demy 8vo, cloth, 24s.

Coleridge (M. E.).—The Seven Sleepers of Ephesus. Cloth, 1s. 6d.

Collins (C. Allston).—The Bar Sinister. Post 8vo, boards, 2s.

Collins (John Churton, M.A.), Books by.
Illustrations of Tennyson. Crown 8vo, cloth extra, 6s.
Jonathan Swift: A Biographical and Critical Study. Crown 8vo, cloth extra, 8s.

Collins (Mortimer and Frances), Novels by.
Crown 8vo, cloth extra, 3s. 6d. each; post 8vo, illustrated boards, 2s. each.

From Midnight to Midnight.	Blacksmith and Scholar.	
Transmigration.	You Play me False.	A Village Comedy.

Post 8vo, illustrated boards, 2s. each.
Sweet Anne Page. | A Fight with Fortune. | Sweet and Twenty. | Frances.

Collins (Wilkie), Novels by.
Crown 8vo, cloth extra, 3s. 6d. each; post 8vo, illustrated boards, 2s. each; cloth limp, 2s. 6d. each.
Antonina. With a Frontispiece by Sir JOHN GILBERT, R.A.
Basil. Illustrated by Sir JOHN GILBERT, R.A., and J. MAHONEY.
Hide and Seek. Illustrated by Sir JOHN GILBERT, R.A., and J. MAHONEY.
After Dark. With Illustrations by A. B. HOUGHTON. | The Two Destinies.
The Dead Secret. With a Frontispiece by Sir JOHN GILBERT, R.A.
Queen of Hearts. With a Frontispiece by Sir JOHN GILBERT, R.A.
The Woman in White. With Illustrations by Sir JOHN GILBERT, R.A., and F. A. FRASER.
No Name. With Illustrations by Sir J. E. MILLAIS, R.A., and A. W. COOPER.
My Miscellanies. With a Steel-plate Portrait of WILKIE COLLINS.
Armadale. With Illustrations by G. H. THOMAS.
The Moonstone. With Illustrations by G. DU MAURIER and F. A. FRASER.
Man and Wife. With Illustrations by WILLIAM SMALL.
Poor Miss Finch. Illustrated by G. DU MAURIER and EDWARD HUGHES.
Miss or Mrs.? With Illustrations by S. L. FILDES, R.A., and HENRY WOODS, A.R.A.
The New Magdalen. Illustrated by G. DU MAURIER and C. S. REINHARDT.
The Frozen Deep. Illustrated by G. DU MAURIER and J. MAHONEY.
The Law and the Lady. With Illustrations by S. L. FILDES, R.A., and SYDNEY HALL.
The Haunted Hotel. With Illustrations by ARTHUR HOPKINS.

The Fallen Leaves.	Heart and Science.	The Evil Genius.
Jezebel's Daughter.	'I Say No.'	Little Novels. Frontis.
The Black Robe.	A Rogue's Life.	The Legacy of Cain.

Blind Love. With a Preface by Sir WALTER BESANT, and Illustrations by A. FORESTIER.

POPULAR EDITIONS. Medium 8vo, 6d. each; cloth, 1s. each.
The Woman in White. | The Moonstone.

The Woman in White and The Moonstone in One Volume, medium 8vo, cloth, 2s.

Colman's (George) Humorous Works: 'Broad Grins,' 'My Night-
gown and Slippers,' &c. With Life and Frontispiece. Crown 8vo, cloth extra, 7s. 6d.

Colquhoun (M. J.).—Every Inch a Soldier. Post 8vo, boards, 2s.

Colt-breaking, Hints on. By W. M. HUTCHISON. Cr. 8vo, cl., 3s. 6d.

Convalescent Cookery. By CATHERINE RYAN. Cr. 8vo, 1s. ; cl., 1s. 6d.

Conway (Moncure D.), Works by.
Demonology and Devil-Lore. With 65 Illustrations. Two Vols., demy 8vo, cloth, 28s.
George Washington's Rules of Civility. Fcap. 8vo, Japanese vellum, 2s. 6d.

Cook (Dutton), Novels by.
Paul Foster's Daughter. Crown 8vo, cloth extra, 3s. 6d. ; post 8vo, illustrated boards, 2s.
Leo. Post 8vo, illustrated boards, 2s.

Cooper (Edward H.).—Geoffory Hamilton. Cr. 8vo, cloth, 3s. 6d.

Cornwall.—Popular Romances of the West of England; or, The
Drolls, Traditions, and Superstitions of Old Cornwall. Collected by ROBERT HUNT, F.R.S. With
two Steel Plates by GEORGE CRUIKSHANK. Crown 8vo, cloth, 7s. 6d.

Cotes (V. Cecil).—Two Girls on a Barge. With 44 Illustrations by
F. H. TOWNSEND. Post 8vo, cloth, 2s. 6d.

Craddock (C. Egbert), Stories by.
The Prophet of the Great Smoky Mountains. Post 8vo, illustrated boards, 2s.
His Vanished Star. Crown 8vo, cloth extra, 3s. 6d.

Cram (Ralph Adams).—Black Spirits and White. Fcap. 8vo, cloth 1s. 6d.

Crellin (H. N.) Books by.
Romances of the Old Seraglio. With 28 Illustrations by S. L. WOOD. Crown 8vo, cloth, 3s. 6d.
Tales of the Caliph. Crown 8vo, cloth, 2s.
The Nazarenes: A Drama. Crown 8vo, 1s.

Crim (Matt.).—Adventures of a Fair Rebel. Crown 8vo, cloth extra, with a Frontispiece by DAN. BEARD, 3s. 6d. ; post 8vo, illustrated boards, 2s.

Crockett (S. R.) and others. — Tales of Our Coast. By S. R. CROCKETT, GILBERT PARKER, HAROLD FREDERIC, 'Q.,' and W. CLARK RUSSELL. With 12 Illustrations by FRANK BRANGWYN. Crown 8vo, cloth, 3s. 6d. [Shortly.

Croker (Mrs. B. M.), Novels by. Crown 8vo, cloth extra, 3s. 6d. each ; post 8vo, illustrated boards 2s. each ; cloth limp, 2s. 6d. each.
Pretty Miss Neville. | Diana Barrington. | A Family Likeness.
A Bird of Passage. | Proper Pride. | 'To Let.'
Village Tales and Jungle Tragedies.
Crown 8vo, cloth extra, 3s. 6d. each.
Mr. Jervis. | The Real Lady Hilda.
Married or Single? Three Vols., crown 8vo, 15s. net.

Cruikshank's Comic Almanack. Complete in TWO SERIES: The FIRST, from 1835 to 1843; the SECOND, from 1844 to 1853. A Gathering of the Best Humour of THACKERAY, HOOD, MAYHEW, ALBERT SMITH, A'BECKETT, ROBERT BROUGH, &c. With numerous Steel Engravings and Woodcuts by GEORGE CRUIKSHANK, HINE, LANDELLS, &c. Two Vols., crown 8vo, cloth gilt, 7s. 6d. each.
The Life of George Cruikshank. By BLANCHARD JERROLD. With 84 Illustrations and a Bibliography. Crown 8vo, cloth extra, 6s.

Cumming (C. F. Gordon), Works by. Demy 8vo, cl. ex., 8s. 6d. ea.
In the Hebrides. With an Autotype Frontispiece and 23 Illustrations.
In the Himalayas and on the Indian Plains. With 42 Illustrations.
Two Happy Years in Ceylon. With 29 Illustrations.
Via Cornwall to Egypt. With a Photogravure Frontispiece. Demy 8vo, cloth, 7s. 6d.

Cussans (John E.).—A Handbook of Heraldry; with Instructions for Tracing Pedigrees and Deciphering Ancient MSS., &c. Fourth Edition, revised, with 408 Woodcuts and 2 Coloured Plates. Crown 8vo, cloth extra, 6s.

Cyples (W.).—Hearts of Gold. Cr. 8vo, cl., 3s. 6d. ; post 8vo, bds., 2s.

Daniel (George).—Merrie England in the Olden Time. With Illustrations by ROBERT CRUIKSHANK. Crown 8vo, cloth extra, 3s. 6d.

Daudet (Alphonse).—The Evangelist; or, Port Salvation. Crown 8vo, cloth extra, 3s. 6d. ; post 8vo, illustrated boards, 2s.

Davenant (Francis, M.A.).—Hints for Parents on the Choice of a Profession for their Sons when Starting in Life. Crown 8vo, 1s. ; cloth, 1s. 6d.

Davidson (Hugh Coleman).—Mr. Sadler's Daughters. With a Frontispiece by STANLEY WOOD. Crown 8vo, cloth extra, 3s. 6d.

Davies (Dr. N. E. Yorke-), Works by. Cr. 8vo, 1s. ea.; cl., 1s. 6d. ea.
One Thousand Medical Maxims and Surgical Hints.
Nursery Hints: A Mother's Guide in Health and Disease.
Foods for the Fat: A Treatise on Corpulency, and a Dietary for its Cure.
Aids to Long Life. Crown 8vo, 2s. ; cloth limp, 2s. 6d.

Davies' (Sir John) Complete Poetical Works. Collected and Edited, with Introduction and Notes, by Rev. A. B. GROSART, D.D. Two Vols., crown 8vo, cloth, 12s.

Dawson (Erasmus, M.B.).—The Fountain of Youth. Crown 8vo, cloth extra, with Two Illustrations by HUME NISBET, 3s. 6d. ; post 8vo, illustrated boards, 2s.

De Guerin (Maurice), The Journal of. Edited by G. S. TREBUTIEN. With a Memoir by SAINTE-BEUVE. Translated from the 20th French Edition by JESSIE P. FROTHINGHAM. Fcap. 8vo, half-bound, 2s. 6d.

De Maistre (Xavier).—A Journey Round my Room. Translated by Sir HENRY ATTWELL. Post 8vo, cloth limp, 2s. 6d.

De Mille (James).—A Castle in Spain. Crown 8vo, cloth extra, with a Frontispiece 3s. 6d. ; post 8vo, illustrated boards, 2s.

Derby (The) : The Blue Ribbon of the Turf. With Brief Accounts of THE OAKS. By LOUIS HENRY CURZON. Crown 8vo, cloth limp, 2s. 6d.

Derwent (Leith), Novels by. Cr. 8vo, cl., 3s. 6d. ea.; post 8vo, 2s. ea.
Our Lady of Tears. | Circe's Lovers.

Dewar (T. R.).—A Ramble Round the Globe. With 220 Illustrations. Crown 8vo, cloth extra, 7s. 6d.

Dickens (Charles), Novels by. Post 8vo, illustrated boards, 2s. each.
Sketches by Boz. | Nicholas Nickleby. | Oliver Twist.

About England with Dickens. By ALFRED RIMMER. With 57 Illustrations by C. A. VANDER-HOOF, ALFRED RIMMER, and others. Square 8vo, cloth extra, 7s. 6d.

Dictionaries.
A Dictionary of Miracles: Imitative, Realistic, and Dogmatic. By the Rev. E. C. BREWER, LL.D. Crown 8vo, cloth extra, 7s. 6d.
The Reader's Handbook of Allusions, References, Plots, and Stories. By the Rev. E. C. BREWER, LL.D. With an ENGLISH BIBLIOGRAPHY. Crown 8vo, cloth extra, 7s. 6d.
Authors and their Works, with the Dates. Crown 8vo, cloth limp, 2s.
Familiar Short Sayings of Great Men. With Historical and Explanatory Notes by SAMUEL A. BENT, A.M. Crown 8vo, cloth extra, 7s. 6d.
The Slang Dictionary: Etymological, Historical, and Anecdotal. Crown 8vo, cloth, 6s. 6d.
Words, Facts, and Phrases: A Dictionary of Curious, Quaint, and Out-of-the-Way Matters. By ELIEZER EDWARDS. Crown 8vo, cloth extra, 7s. 6d.

Diderot.—The Paradox of Acting. Translated, with Notes, by WALTER HERRIES POLLOCK. With Preface by Sir HENRY IRVING. Crown 8vo, parchment, 4s. 6d.

Dobson (Austin), Works by.
Thomas Bewick and his Pupils. With 95 Illustrations. Square 8vo, cloth, 6s.
Four Frenchwomen. With Four Portraits. Crown 8vo, buckram, gilt top, 6s.
Eighteenth Century Vignettes. TWO SERIES Crown 8vo, buckram, 6s. each.—A THIRD SERIES is in preparation.

Dobson (W. T.).—Poetical Ingenuities and Eccentricities. Post 8vo, cloth limp, 2s. 6d.

Donovan (Dick), Detective Stories by.
Post 8vo, illustrated boards, 2s. each; cloth limp, 2s. 6d. each.
The Man-Hunter. | Wanted. | A Detective's Triumphs.
Caught at Last. | In the Grip of the Law.
Tracked and Taken. | From Information Received.
Who Poisoned Hetty Duncan? | Link by Link. | Dark Deeds.
Suspicion Aroused. | Riddles Read.

Crown 8vo, cloth extra, 3s. 6d. each; post 8vo, illustrated boards, 2s. each; cloth, 2s. 6d. each.
The Man from Manchester. With 23 Illustrations.
Tracked to Doom. With Six full-page Illustrations by GORDON BROWNE.

The Mystery of Jamaica Terrace. Crown 8vo, cloth, 3s. 6d.

Doyle (A. Conan).—The Firm of Girdlestone. Cr. 8vo, cl., 3s. 6d.

Dramatists, The Old. Crown 8vo, cl. ex., with Portraits, 6s. per Vol.
Ben Jonson's Works. With Notes, Critical and Explanatory, and a Biographical Memoir by WILLIAM GIFFORD. Edited by Colonel CUNNINGHAM. Three Vols.
Chapman's Works. Three Vols. Vol. I. contains the Plays complete; Vol. II., Poems and Minor Translations, with an Essay by A. C. SWINBURNE; Vol. III., Translations of the Iliad and Odyssey.
Marlowe's Works. Edited, with Notes, by Colonel CUNNINGHAM. One Vol.
Massinger's Plays. From GIFFORD'S Text. Edited by Colonel CUNNINGHAM. One Vol.

Duncan (Sara Jeannette: Mrs. EVERARD COTES), Works by.
Crown 8vo, cloth extra, 7s. 6d. each.
A Social Departure. With 111 Illustrations by F. H. TOWNSEND.
An American Girl in London. With 80 Illustrations by F. H. TOWNSEND.
The Simple Adventures of a Memsahib. With 37 Illustrations by F. H. TOWNSEND.

Crown 8vo, cloth extra, 3s. 6d. each.
A Daughter of To-Day. | Vernon's Aunt. With 47 Illustrations by HAL HURST.

Dyer (T. F. Thiselton).—The Folk-Lore of Plants. Cr. 8vo, cl., 6s.

Early English Poets. Edited, with Introductions and Annotations, by Rev. A. B. GROSART, D.D. Crown 8vo, cloth boards, 6s. per Volume.
Fletcher's (Giles) Complete Poems. One Vol.
Davies' (Sir John) Complete Poetical Works. Two Vols.
Herrick's (Robert) Complete Collected Poems. Three Vols.
Sidney's (Sir Philip) Complete Poetical Works. Three Vols.

Edgcumbe (Sir E. R. Pearce).—Zephyrus: A Holiday in Brazil and on the River Plate. With 41 Illustrations. Crown 8vo, cloth extra, 5s.

Edison, The Life and Inventions of Thomas A. By W. K. L. and ANTONIA DICKSON. With 200 Illustrations by R. F. OUTCALT, &c. Demy 4to, cloth gilt, 8

Edwardes (Mrs. Annie), Novels by.
Post 8vo, illustrated boards, 2s. each.
Archie Lovell. | A Point of Honour.

Edwards (Eliezer).—Words, Facts, and Phrases: A Dictionary
of Curious Quaint, and Out-of-the-Way Matters. Crown 8vo, cloth, 7s. 6d.

Edwards (M. Betham-), Novels by.
Kitty. Post 8vo, boards, 2s.; cloth, 2s. 6d. | Felicia. Post 8vo, illustrated boards, 2s.

Egerton (Rev. J. C., M.A.). — Sussex Folk and Sussex Ways.
With Introduction by Rev. Dr. H. WACE, and Four Illustrations. Crown 8vo, cloth extra, 5s.

Eggleston (Edward).—Roxy: A Novel. Post 8vo, illust. boards, 2s.

Englishman's House, The: A Practical Guide for Selecting or Build-
ing a House. By C. J. RICHARDSON. Coloured Frontispiece and 534 Illusts. Cr. 8vo, cloth, 7s. 6d.

Ewald (Alex. Charles, F.S.A.), Works by.
The Life and Times of Prince Charles Stuart, Count of Albany (THE YOUNG PRETEN-
DER). With a Portrait. Crown 8vo, cloth extra, 7s. 6d.
Stories from the State Papers. With Autotype Frontispiece. Crown 8vo, cloth, 6s.

Eyes, Our: How to Preserve Them. By JOHN BROWNING. Cr. 8vo, 1s.

Familiar Short Sayings of Great Men. By SAMUEL ARTHUR BENT,
A.M. Fifth Edition, Revised and Enlarged. Crown 8vo, cloth extra, 7s. 6d.

Faraday (Michael), Works by. Post 8vo, cloth extra, 4s. 6d. each.
The Chemical History of a Candle: Lectures delivered before a Juvenile Audience. Edited
by WILLIAM CROOKES, F.C.S. With numerous Illustrations.
On the Various Forces of Nature, and their Relations to each other. Edited by
WILLIAM CROOKES, F.C.S. With Illustrations.

Farrer (J. Anson), Works by.
Military Manners and Customs. Crown 8vo, cloth extra, 6s.
War: Three Essays, reprinted from 'Military Manners and Customs.' Crown 8vo, 1s.; cloth, 1s. 6d.

Fenn (G. Manville), Novels by.
Crown 8vo, cloth extra, 3s. 6d. each; post 8vo, illustrated boards, 2s. each.
The New Mistress. | Witness to the Deed.
The Tiger Lily: A Tale of Two Passions.

The White Virgin. Crown 8vo, cloth extra, 3s. 6d.

Fin=Bec.—The Cupboard Papers: Observations on the Art of Living
and Dining. Post 8vo, cloth limp, 2s. 6d.

Fireworks, The Complete Art of Making; or, The Pyrotechnist's
Treasury. By THOMAS KENTISH. With 267 Illustrations. Crown 8vo, cloth, 5s.

First Book, My. By WALTER BESANT, JAMES PAYN, W. CLARK RUS-
SELL, GRANT ALLEN, HALL CAINE, GEORGE R. SIMS, RUDYARD KIPLING, A. CONAN DOYLE,
M. E. BRADDON, F. W. ROBINSON, H. RIDER HAGGARD, R. M. BALLANTYNE, I. ZANGWILL,
MORLEY ROBERTS, D. CHRISTIE MURRAY, MARY CORELLI, J. K. JEROME, JOHN STRANGE
WINTER, BRET HARTE, 'Q.,' ROBERT BUCHANAN, and R. L. STEVENSON. With a Prefatory Story
by JEROME K. JEROME, and 185 Illustrations. Small demy 8vo, cloth extra, 7s. 6d.

Fitzgerald (Percy), Works by.
The World Behind the Scenes. Crown 8vo, cloth extra, 3s. 6d.
Little Essays: Passages from the Letters of CHARLES LAMB. Post 8vo, cloth, 2s. 6d.
A Day's Tour: A Journey through France and Belgium. With Sketches. Crown 4to, 1s.
Fatal Zero. Crown 8vo, cloth extra, 3s. 6d.; post 8vo, illustrated boards, 2s.

Post 8vo, illustrated boards, 2s. each.
Bella Donna. | The Lady of Brantome. | The Second Mrs. Tillotson.
Polly. | Never Forgotten. | Seventy-five Brooke Street.

The Life of James Boswell (of Auchinleck). With Illusts. Two Vols., demy 8vo, cloth, 24s.
The Savoy Opera. With 60 Illustrations and Portraits. Crown 8vo, cloth, 3s. 6d.
Sir Henry Irving: Twenty Years at the Lyceum. With Portrait. Crown 8vo, 1s.; cloth, 1s. 6d.

Flammarion (Camille), Works by.
Popular Astronomy: A General Description of the Heavens. Translated by J. ELLARD GORE,
F.R.A.S. With Three Plates and 288 Illustrations. Medium 8vo, cloth, 16s.
Urania: A Romance. With 87 Illustrations. Crown 8vo, cloth extra, 5s.

Fletcher's (Giles, B.D.) Complete Poems: Christ's Victorie in
Heaven, Christ's Victorie on Earth, Christ's Triumph over Death, and Minor Poems. With Notes by
Rev. A. B. GROSART, D.D. Crown 8vo, cloth boards, 6s.

Fonblanque (Albany).—Filthy Lucre. Post 8vo, illust. boards, 2s.

Francillon (R. E.), Novels by.
Crown 8vo, cloth extra, 3s. 6d. each; post 8vo, illustrated boards, 2s. each.

One by One. | **A Real Queen.** | **A Dog and his Shadow.**
Ropes of Sand. Illustrated.

Post 8vo, illustrated boards, 2s. each.

Queen Cophetua. | **Olympia.** | **Romances of the Law.** | **King or Knave?**

Jack Doyle's Daughter. Crown 8vo, cloth, 3s. 6d.
Esther's Glove. Fcap. 8vo, picture cover, 1s.

Frederic (Harold), Novels by. Post 8vo, illust. boards, 2s. each.
Seth's Brother's Wife. | **The Lawton Girl.**

French Literature, A History of. By HENRY VAN LAUN. Three
Vols., demy 8vo, cloth boards, 7s. 6d. each.

Friswell (Hain).—One of Two: A Novel. Post 8vo, illust. bds., 2s.

Frost (Thomas), Works by. Crown 8vo, cloth extra, 3s. 6d. each.
Circus Life and Circus Celebrities. | **Lives of the Conjurers.**
The Old Showmen and the Old London Fairs.

Fry's (Herbert) Royal Guide to the London Charities. Edited
by JOHN LANE. Published Annually. Crown 8vo, cloth, 1s. 6d.

Gardening Books. Post 8vo, 1s. each; cloth limp. 1s. 6d. each.
A Year's Work in Garden and Greenhouse. By GEORGE GLENNY.
Household Horticulture. By TOM and JANE JERROLD. Illustrated.
The Garden that Paid the Rent. By TOM JERROLD.

My Garden Wild. By FRANCIS G. HEATH. Crown 8vo, cloth extra, 6s.

Gardner (Mrs. Alan).—Rifle and Spear with the Rajpoots: Being
the Narrative of a Winter's Travel and Sport in Northern India. With numerous Illustrations by the Author and F. H. TOWNSEND. Demy 4to, half-bound, 21s.

Garrett (Edward).—The Capel Girls: A Novel. Crown 8vo, cloth
extra, with two Illustrations, 3s. 6d.; post 8vo, illustrated boards, 2s.

Gaulot (Paul).—The Red Shirts: A Story of the Revolution. Trans-
lated by JOHN DE VILLIERS. With a Frontispiece by STANLEY WOOD. Crown 8vo, cloth, 3s. 6d.

Gentleman's Magazine, The. 1s. Monthly. Contains Stories,
Articles upon Literature, Science, Biography, and Art, and 'Table Talk' by SYLVANUS URBAN.
. Bound Volumes for recent years kept in stock, 8s. 6d. each. Cases for binding, 2s.

Gentleman's Annual, The. Published Annually in November. 1s.

German Popular Stories. Collected by the Brothers GRIMM and
Translated by EDGAR TAYLOR. With Introduction by JOHN RUSKIN, and 22 Steel Plates after GEORGE CRUIKSHANK. Square 8vo, cloth, 6s. 6d.; gilt edges, 7s. 6d.

Gibbon (Charles), Novels by.
Crown 8vo, cloth extra, 3s. 6d. each; post 8vo, Illustrated boards, 2s. each.

Robin Gray. Frontispiece. | **The Golden Shaft.** Frontispiece. | **Loving a Dream.**

Post 8vo, illustrated boards, 2s. each.

The Flower of the Forest.	**In Love and War.**
The Dead Heart.	**A Heart's Problem.**
For Lack of Gold.	**By Mead and Stream.**
What Will the World Say?	**The Braes of Yarrow.**
For the King. | **A Hard Knot.**	**Fancy Free.** | **Of High Degree.**
Queen of the Meadow.	**In Honour Bound.**
In Pastures Green.	**Heart's Delight.** | **Blood-Money.**

Gibney (Somerville).—Sentenced! Crown 8vo, 1s.; cloth, 1s. 6d.

Gilbert (W. S.), Original Plays by. In Three Series, 2s. 6d. each.
The FIRST SERIES contains: The Wicked World—Pygmalion and Galatea—Charity—The Princess—The Palace of Truth—Trial by Jury.
The SECOND SERIES: Broken Hearts—Engaged—Sweethearts—Gretchen—Dan'l Druce—Tom Cobb—H.M.S. 'Pinafore'—The Sorcerer—The Pirates of Penzance.
The THIRD SERIES: Comedy and Tragedy—Foggerty's Fairy—Rosencrantz and Guildenstern—Patience—Princess Ida—The Mikado—Ruddigore—The Yeomen of the Guard—The Gondoliers—The Mountebanks—Utopia.

Eight Original Comic Operas written by W. S. GILBERT. Containing: The Sorcerer—H.M.S. 'Pinafore'—The Pirates of Penzance—Iolanthe—Patience—Princess Ida—The Mikado—Trial by Jury. Demy 8vo, cloth limp, 2s. 6d.

The Gilbert and Sullivan Birthday Book: Quotations for Every Day in the Year, selected from Plays by W. S. GILBERT set to Music by Sir A. SULLIVAN. Compiled by ALEX. WATSON. Royal 16mo, Japanese leather, 2s. 6d.

Gilbert (William), Novels by. Post 8vo, illustrated bds., 2s. each.
Dr. Austin's Guests. | James Duke, Costermonger.
The Wizard of the Mountain.

Glanville (Ernest), Novels by.
Crown 8vo, cloth extra, 3s. 6d. each ; post 8vo, illustrated boards, 2s. each.
The Lost Heiress : A Tale of Love, Battle, and Adventure. With Two Illustrations by H. NISBET.
The Fossicker : A Romance of Mashonaland. With Two Illustrations by HUME NISBET.
A Fair Colonist. With a Frontispiece by STANLEY WOOD.

The Golden Rock. With a Frontispiece by STANLEY WOOD. Crown 8vo, cloth extra, 3s. 6d.
Kloof Yarns. Crown 8vo, picture cover, 1s. ; cloth, 1s. 6d. [Shortly.

Glenny (George).—A Year's Work in Garden and Greenhouse :
Practical Advice as to the Management of the Flower, Fruit, and Frame Garden. Post 8vo, 1s. ; cloth, 1s. 6d.

Godwin (William).—Lives of the Necromancers. Post 8vo, cl., 2s.

Golden Treasury of Thought, The : An Encyclopædia of QUOTA-
TIONS. Edited by THEODORE TAYLOR. Crown 8vo, cloth gilt, 7s. 6d.

Gontaut, Memoirs of the Duchesse de (Gouvernante to the Chil-
dren of France), 1773-1836. With Two Photogravures. Two Vols., demy 8vo, cloth extra, 21s.

Goodman (E. J.).—The Fate of Herbert Wayne. Cr. 8vo, 3s. 6d.

Graham (Leonard).—The Professor's Wife : A Story. Fcp. 8vo, 1s.

Greeks and Romans, The Life of the, described from Antique
Monuments. By ERNST GUHL and W. KONER. Edited by Dr. F. HUEFFER. With 545 Illustrations. Large crown 8vo, cloth extra, 7s. 6d.

Greenwood (James), Works by. Crown 8vo, cloth extra, 3s. 6d. each.
The Wilds of London. | Low-Life Deeps.

Greville (Henry), Novels by.
Nikanor. Translated by ELIZA E. CHASE. Post 8vo, illustrated boards, 2s.
A Noble Woman. Crown 8vo, cloth extra, 5s. ; post 8vo, illustrated boards, 2s.

Griffith (Cecil).—Corinthia Marazion : A Novel. Crown 8vo, cloth
extra, 3s. 6d. ; post 8vo, illustrated boards, 2s.

Grundy (Sydney).—The Days of his Vanity : A Passage in the
Life of a Young Man. Crown 8vo, cloth extra, 3s. 6d. ; post 8vo, illustrated boards, 2s.

Habberton (John, Author of ' Helen's Babies '), **Novels by.**
Post 8vo, illustrated boards, 2s. each : cloth limp, 2s. 6d. each.
Brueton's Bayou. | Country Luck.

Hair, The : Its Treatment in Health, Weakness, and Disease. Translated from the German of Dr. J. PINCUS. Crown 8vo, 1s. ; cloth, 1s. 6d.

Hake (Dr. Thomas Gordon), Poems by. Cr. 8vo, cl. ex., 6s. each.
New Symbols. | Legends of the Morrow. | The Serpent Play.

Maiden Ecstasy. Small 4to, cloth extra, 8s.

Hall (Owen).—The Track of a Storm. Crown 8vo, cloth, 6s.

Hall (Mrs. S. C.).—Sketches of Irish Character. With numerous
Illustrations on Steel and Wood by MACLISE, GILBERT, HARVEY, and GEORGE CRUIKSHANK.
Small demy 8vo, cloth extra, 7s. 6d.

Halliday (Andrew).—Every-day Papers. Post 8vo, boards, 2s.

Handwriting, The Philosophy of. With over 100 Facsimiles and
Explanatory Text. By DON FELIX DE SALAMANCA. Post 8vo, cloth limp, 2s. 6d.

Hanky-Panky : Easy and Difficult Tricks, White Magic, Sleight of
Hand, &c. Edited by W. H. CREMER. With 200 Illustrations. Crown 8vo, cloth extra, 4s. 6d.

Hardy (Lady Duffus).—Paul Wynter's Sacrifice. Post 8vo, bds., 2s.

Hardy (Thomas).—Under the Greenwood Tree. Crown 8vo, cloth
extra, with Portrait and 15 Illustrations, 3s. 6d. ; post 8vo, illustrated boards, 2s. cloth limp, 2s. 6d.

Harper (Charles G.), Works by. Demy 8vo, cloth extra, 16s. each.
The Brighton Road. With Photogravure Frontispiece and 90 Illustrations.
From Paddington to Penzance : The Record of a Summer Tramp. With 105 Illustrations.

Harwood (J. Berwick).—The Tenth Earl. Post 8vo, boards, 2s.

Harte's (Bret) Collected Works. Revised by the Author. LIBRARY
EDITION, in Eight Volumes, crown 8vo, cloth extra, 6s. each.
Vol. I. COMPLETE POETICAL AND DRAMATIC WORKS. With Steel-plate Portrait.
" II. THE LUCK OF ROARING CAMP—BOHEMIAN PAPERS—AMERICAN LEGENDS.
" III. TALES OF THE ARGONAUTS—EASTERN SKETCHES.
" IV. GABRIEL CONROY. | Vol. V. STORIES—CONDENSED NOVELS, &c.
" VI. TALES OF THE PACIFIC SLOPE.
" VII. TALES OF THE PACIFIC SLOPE—II. With Portrait by JOHN PETTIE, R.A.
" VIII. TALES OF THE PINE AND THE CYPRESS.

The Select Works of Bret Harte, in Prose and Poetry. With Introductory Essay by J. M.
BELLEW, Portrait of the Author, and 50 Illustrations. Crown 8vo, cloth extra, 7s. 6d.
Bret Harte's Poetical Works. Printed on hand-made paper. Crown 8vo, buckram, 4s. 6d.
The Queen of the Pirate Isle. With 28 Original Drawings by KATE GREENAWAY, reproduced
in Colours by EDMUND EVANS. Small 4to, cloth, 5s.

Crown 8vo, cloth extra, 3s. 6d. each; post 8vo, picture boards, 2s. each.
A Waif of the Plains. With 60 Illustrations by STANLEY L. WOOD.
A Ward of the Golden Gate. With 59 Illustrations by STANLEY L. WOOD.

Crown 8vo, cloth extra, 3s. 6d. each.
A Sappho of Green Springs, &c. With Two Illustrations by HUME NISBET.
Colonel Starbottle's Client, and Some Other People. With a Frontispiece.
Susy: A Novel. With Frontispiece and Vignette by J. A. CHRISTIE.
Sally Dows, &c. With 47 Illustrations by W. D. ALMOND and others.
A Protegee of Jack Hamlin's. With 26 Illustrations by W. SMALL and others.
The Bell-Ringer of Angel's, &c. With 39 Illustrations by DUDLEY HARDY and others
Clarence: A Story of the American War. With Eight Illustrations by A. JULE GOODMAN.

Post 8vo, illustrate | boards, 2s. each.
Gabriel Conroy. | **The Luck of Roaring Camp,** &c.
An Heiress of Red Dog, &c. | **Californian Stories.**

Post 8vo, illustrated boards, 2s. each; cloth, 2s. 6d. each.
Flip. | **Maruja.** | **A Phyllis of the Sierras.**

Fcap. 8vo, picture cover, 1s. each.
Snow-Bound at Eagle's. | **Jeff Briggs's Love Story.**

Haweis (Mrs. H. R.), Books by.
The Art of Beauty. With Coloured Frontispiece and 91 Illustrations. Square 8vo, cloth bds., 6s.
The Art of Decoration. With Coloured Frontispiece and 74 Illustrations. Sq. 8vo, cloth bds., 6s.
The Art of Dress. With 32 Illustrations. Post 8vo, 1s.; cloth, 1s. 6d.
Chaucer for Schools. Demy 8vo, cloth limp, 2s. 6d.
Chaucer for Children. With 38 Illustrations (8 Coloured). Crown 4to, cloth extra, 3s. 6d.

Haweis (Rev. H. R., M.A.), Books by.
American Humorists: WASHINGTON IRVING, OLIVER WENDELL HOLMES, JAMES RUSSELL
LOWELL, ARTEMUS WARD, MARK TWAIN, and BRET HARTE. Third Edition. Crown 8vo,
cloth extra, 6s.
Travel and Talk, 1885, 1893, 1895: America—New Zealand—Tasmania—Ceylon. With Pho-
togravure Frontispieces. Two Vols., crown 8vo, cloth. 21s. [Shortly.

Hawthorne (Julian), Novels by.
Crown 8vo, cloth extra, 3s. 6d. each 'post 8vo, illustrated boards, 2s. each.
Garth. | **Ellice Quentin.** | **Beatrix Randolph.** With Four Illusts.
Sebastian Strome. | **David Poindexter's Disappearance.**
Fortune's Fool. | **Dust.** Four Illusts. | **The Spectre of the Camera.**

Post 8vo, illustrated boards, 2s. each.
Miss Cadogna. | **Love—or a Name.**
Mrs. Gainsborough's Diamonds. Fcap. 8vo, illustrated cover, 1s.

Hawthorne (Nathaniel).—Our Old Home. Annotated with Pas-
sages from the Author's Note-books, and Illustrated with 31 Photogravures. Two Vols., cr. 8vo, 15s.

Heath (Francis George).—My Garden Wild, and What I Grew
There. Crown 8vo, cloth extra, gilt edges, 6s.

Helps (Sir Arthur), Works by. Post 8vo, cloth limp, 2s. 6d. each.
Animals and their Masters. | **Social Pressure.**
Ivan de Biron: A Novel. Crown 8vo, cloth extra, 3s. 6d.; post 8vo, illustrated boards, 2s.

Henderson (Isaac). — Agatha Page: A Novel. Cr. 8vo, cl., 3s. 6d.

Henty (G. A.), Novels by.
Rujub the Juggler. With Eight Illustrations by STANLEY L. WOOD. Crown 8vo, cloth, 3s. 6d.;
post 8vo, illustrated boards, 2s.
Dorothy's Double. Crown 8vo, cloth, 3s. 6d.

Herman (Henry).—A Leading Lady. Post 8vo, bds., 2s.; cl., 2s. 6d.

**Herrick's (Robert) Hesperides, Noble Numbers, and Complete
Collected Poems.** With Memorial-Introduction and Notes by the Rev. A. B. GROSART, D.D.,
Steel Portrait, &c. Three Vols., crown 8vo, cloth boards, 18s.

Hertzka (Dr. Theodor).—Freeland: A Social Anticipation. Translated by ARTHUR RANSOM. Crown 8vo, cloth extra, 6s.

Hesse=Wartegg (Chevalier Ernst von).— Tunis: The Land and the People. With 22 Illustrations. Crown 8vo, cloth extra, 3s. 6d.

Hill (Headon).—Zambra the Detective. Post 8vo, bds., 2s.; cl., 2s. 6d.

Hill (John), Works by.
Treason-Felony. Post 8vo, boards, 2s. | The Common Ancestor. Cr. 8vo, cloth, 3s. 6d.

Hindley (Charles), Works by.
Tavern Anecdotes and Sayings: Including Reminiscences connected with Coffee Houses, Clubs, &c. With Illustrations. Crown 8vo, cloth extra, 3s. 6d.
The Life and Adventures of a Cheap Jack. Crown 8vo, cloth extra, 3s. 6d.

Hodges (Sydney).—When Leaves were Green. 3 vols., 15s. net.

Hoey (Mrs. Cashel).—The Lover's Creed. Post 8vo, boards, 2s.

Hollingshead (John).—Niagara Spray. Crown 8vo, 1s.

Holmes (Gordon, M.D.)—The Science of Voice Production and Voice Preservation. Crown 8vo, 1s.; cloth, 1s. 6d.

Holmes (Oliver Wendell), Works by.
The Autocrat of the Breakfast-Table. Illustrated by J. GORDON THOMSON. Post 8vo, cloth limp, 2s. 6d.— Another Edition, post 8vo, cloth, 2s.
The Autocrat of the Breakfast-Table and The Professor at the Breakfast-Table. In One Vol. Post 8vo, half-bound, 2s.

Hood's (Thomas) Choice Works in Prose and Verse. With Life of the Author, Portrait, and 200 Illustrations. Crown 8vo, cloth extra, 7s. 6d.
Hood's Whims and Oddities. With 85 Illustrations. Post 8vo, half-bound, 2s.

Hood (Tom).—From Nowhere to the North Pole: A Noah's Arkæological Narrative. With 25 Illustrations by W. BRUNTON and E. C. BARNES. Cr. 8vo, cloth, 6s.

Hook's (Theodore) Choice Humorous Works; including his Ludicrous Adventures, Bons Mots, Puns, and Hoaxes. With Life of the Author, Portraits, Facsimiles, and Illustrations. Crown 8vo, cloth extra, 7s. 6d.

Hooper (Mrs. Geo.).—The House of Raby. Post 8vo, boards, 2s.

Hopkins (Tighe).—''Twixt Love and Duty.' Post 8vo, boards, 2s.

Horne (R. Hengist). — Orion: An Epic Poem. With Photograph Portrait by SUMMERS. Tenth Edition. Crown 8vo, cloth extra, 7s.

Hungerford (Mrs., Author of ' Molly Bawn '), Novels by.
Post 8vo, illustrated boards, 2s. each; cloth limp, 2s. 6d. each.
A Maiden All Forlorn. | In Durance Vile. | A Mental Struggle.
Marvel. | A Modern Circe.

Crown 8vo, cloth extra, 3s. 6d. each; post 8vo, illustrated boards, 2s. each; cloth limp, 2s. 6d. each.
Lady Verner's Flight. | The Red-House Mystery.

The Three Graces. With 6 Illustrations. Crown 8vo, cloth extra, 3s. 6d.   [Shortly.
The Professor's Experiment. Three Vols., crown 8vo, 15s. net.
A Point of Conscience. Three Vols., crown 8vo, 15s. net.

Hunt's (Leigh) Essays: A Tale for a Chimney Corner, &c. Edited by EDMUND OLLIER. Post 8vo, half-bound, 2s.

Hunt (Mrs. Alfred), Novels by.
Crown 8vo, cloth extra, 3s. 6d. each; post 8vo, illustrated boards, 2s. each.
The Leaden Casket. | Self-Condemned. | That Other Person.

Thornicroft's Model. Post 8vo, boards, 2s. | Mrs. Juliet. Crown 8vo, cloth extra, 3s. 6d.

Hutchison (W. M.).—Hints on Colt=breaking. With 25 Illustrations. Crown 8vo, cloth extra, 3s. 6d.

Hydrophobia: An Account of M. PASTEUR'S System; The Technique of his Method, and Statistics. By RENAUD SUZOR, M.B. Crown 8vo, cloth extra, 6s.

Hyne (C. J. Cutcliffe).—Honour of Thieves. Cr. 8vo, cloth, 3s. 6d.

Idler (The): An Illustrated Magazine. Edited by J. K. JEROME. 1s. Monthly. The First EIGHT VOLS. are now ready, cloth extra, 5s. each; Cases for Binding, 1s. 6d. each.

Impressions (The) of Aureole. Crown 8vo, printed on blush-rose paper and handsomely bound, 6s.

Indoor Paupers. By ONE OF THEM. Crown 8vo, 1s. ; cloth, 1s. 6d.

Ingelow (Jean).—Fated to be Free. Post 8vo, illustrated bds., 2s.

Innkeeper's Handbook (The) and Licensed Victualler's Manual. By J. TREVOR-DAVIES. Crown 8vo, 1s. : cloth, 1s. 6d.

Irish Wit and Humour, Songs of. Collected and Edited by A. PERCEVAL GRAVES. Post 8vo, cloth limp, 2s. 6d.

Irving (Sir Henry) : A Record of over Twenty Years at the Lyceum. By PERCY FITZGERALD. With Portrait. Crown 8vo, 1s.; cloth, 1s. 6d.

James (C. T. C.). — A Romance of the Queen's Hounds. Post 8vo, picture cover, 1s. ; cloth limp, 1s. 6d.

Jameson (William).—My Dead Self. Post 8vo, bds., 2s. ; cl., 2s. 6d.

Japp (Alex. H., LL.D.).—Dramatic Pictures, &c. Cr. 8vo, cloth, 5s.

Jay (Harriett), Novels by. Post 8vo, illustrated boards, 2s. each.
The Dark Colleen. | The Queen of Connaught.

Jefferies (Richard), Works by. Post 8vo, cloth limp, 2s. 6d. each.
Nature near London. | The Life of the Fields. | The Open Air.
** Also the HAND-MADE PAPER EDITION, crown 8vo, buckram, gilt top, 6s. each.

The Eulogy of Richard Jefferies. By Sir WALTER BESANT. With a Photograph Portrait. Crown 8vo, cloth extra, 6s.

Jennings (Henry J.), Works by.
Curiosities of Criticism. Post 8vo, cloth limp, 2s. 6d.
Lord Tennyson : A Biographical Sketch. With Portrait. Post 8vo, 1s.; cloth, 1s. 6d.

Jerome (Jerome K.), Books by.
Stageland. With 64 Illustrations by J. BERNARD PARTRIDGE. Fcap. 4to, picture cover, 1s.
John Ingerfield, &c. With 9 Illusts. by A. S. BOYD and JOHN GULICH. Fcap. 8vo, pic. cov. 1s. 6d.
The Prude's Progress : A Comedy by J. K. JEROME and EDEN PHILLPOTTS. Cr. 8vo, 1s. 6d.

Jerrold (Douglas).—The Barber's Chair; and The Hedgehog Letters. Post 8vo, printed on laid paper and half-bound, 2s.

Jerrold (Tom), Works by. Post 8vo, 1s. ea. ; cloth limp, 1s. 6d. each.
The Garden that Paid the Rent.
Household Horticulture : A Gossip about Flowers. Illustrated.

Jesse (Edward).—Scenes and Occupations of a Country Life. Post 8vo, cloth limp, 2s.

Jones (William, F.S.A.), Works by. Cr. 8vo, cl. extra, 7s. 6d. each.
Finger-Ring Lore : Historical, Legendary, and Anecdotal. With nearly 300 Illustrations. Second Edition, Revised and Enlarged.
Credulities, Past and Present. Including the Sea and Seamen, Miners, Talismans, Word and Letter Divination, Exorcising and Blessing of Animals, Birds, Eggs, Luck, &c. With Frontispiece.
Crowns and Coronations : A History of Regalia. With 100 Illustrations.

Jonson's (Ben) Works. With Notes Critical and Explanatory, and a Biographical Memoir by WILLIAM GIFFORD. Edited by Colonel CUNNINGHAM. Three Vols, crown 8vo, cloth extra, 6s. each.

Josephus, The Complete Works of. Translated by WHISTON. Containing 'The Antiquities of the Jews' and 'The Wars of the Jews.' With 52 Illustrations and Maps, Two Vols., demy 8vo, half-bound, 12s. 6d.

Kempt (Robert).—Pencil and Palette : Chapters on Art and Artists. Post 8vo, cloth limp, 2s. 6d.

Kershaw (Mark). — Colonial Facts and Fictions : Humorous Sketches. Post 8vo, illustrated boards, 2s. ; cloth, 2s. 6d.

Keyser (Arthur).—Cut by the Mess. Crown 8vo, 1s. ; cloth, 1s. 6d.

King (R. Ashe), Novels by. Cr. 8vo, cl., 3s. 6d. ea.; post 8vo, bds., 2s. ea.
A Drawn Game. | 'The Wearing of the Green.'

Post 8vo, illustrated boards, 2s. each.
Passion's Slave. | Bell Barry.

Knight (William, M.R.C.S., and Edward, L.R.C.P.). — The Patient's Vade Mecum: How to Get Most Benefit from Medical Advice. Cr. 8vo, 1s.; cl., 1s. 6d.

Knights (The) of the Lion: A Romance of the Thirteenth Century. Edited, with an Introduction, by the MARQUESS OF LORNE, K.T. Crown 8vo, cloth extra, 6s.

Lamb's (Charles) Complete Works in Prose and Verse, including 'Poetry for Children' and 'Prince Dorus.' Edited, with Notes and Introduction, by R. H. SHEP-HERD. With Two Portraits and Facsimile of the 'Essay on Roast Pig.' Crown 8vo, half-bd., 7s. 6d.
The Essays of Elia. Post 8vo, printed on laid paper and half-bound, 2s.
Little Essays: Sketches and Characters by CHARLES LAMB, selected from his Letters by PERCY FITZGERALD. Post 8vo, cloth limp, 2s. 6d.
The Dramatic Essays of Charles Lamb. With Introduction and Notes by BRANDER MAT-THEWS, and Steel-plate Portrait. Fcap. 8vo, half-bound, 2s. 6d.

Landor (Walter Savage).—Citation and Examination of William Shakspeare, &c., before Sir Thomas Lucy, touching Deer-stealing, 19th September, 1582. To which is added, **A Conference of Master Edmund Spenser** with the Earl of Essex, touching the State of Ireland, 1595. Fcap. 8vo, half-Roxburghe, 2s. 6d.

Lane (Edward William).—The Thousand and One Nights, com-monly called in England **The Arabian Nights' Entertainments.** Translated from the Arabic, with Notes. Illustrated with many hundred Engravings from Designs by HARVEY. Edited by EDWARD STANLEY POOLE. With Preface by STANLEY LANE-POOLE. Three Vols., demy 8vo, cloth, 7s. 6d. ea.

Larwood (Jacob), Works by.
The Story of the London Parks. With Illustrations. Crown 8vo, cloth extra, 3s. 6d.
Anecdotes of the Clergy. Post 8vo, laid paper, half-bound, 2s.
Post 8vo, cloth limp, 2s. 6d. each.
Forensic Anecdotes. | **Theatrical Anecdotes.**

Lehmann (R. C.), Works by. Post 8vo, 1s. each; cloth, 1s. 6d. each.
Harry Fludyer at Cambridge.
Conversational Hints for Young Shooters: A Guide to Polite Talk.

Leigh (Henry S.), Works by.
Carols of Cockayne. Printed on hand-made paper, bound in buckram, 5s.
Jeux d'Esprit. Edited by HENRY S. LEIGH. Post 8vo, cloth limp, 2s. 6d.

Leland (C. Godfrey). — A Manual of Mending and Repairing. With Diagrams. Crown 8vo, cloth, 5s. [Shortly.

Lepelletier (Edmond). — Madame Sans-Gène. Translated from the French by JOHN DE VILLIERS. Crown 8vo, cloth extra, 3s. 6d.

Leys (John).—The Lindsays: A Romance. Post 8vo, illust. bds., 2s.

Lindsay (Harry).—Rhoda Roberts: A Welsh Mining Story. Crown 8vo, cloth, 3s. 6d.

Linton (E. Lynn), Works by.
Crown 8vo, cloth extra, 3s. 6d. each; post 8vo, illustrated boards, 2s. each.
Patricia Kemball. | **Ione.** | **Under which Lord?** With 12 Illustrations.
The Atonement of Leam Dundas. | **'My Love!'** | **Sowing the Wind.**
The World Well Lost. With 12 Illusts. | **Paston Carew,** Millionaire and Miser.
The One Too Many.
Post 8vo, illustrated boards, 2s. each.
The Rebel of the Family. | **With a Silken Thread.**
Post 8vo, cloth limp, 2s. 6d. each.
Witch Stories. | **Ourselves:** Essays on Women.
Freeshooting: Extracts from the Works of Mrs. LYNN LINTON.

Lucy (Henry W.).—Gideon Fleyce: A Novel. Crown 8vo, cloth extra, 3s. 6d.; post 8vo, illustrated boards, 2s.

Macalpine (Avery), Novels by.
Teresa Itasca. Crown 8vo, cloth extra, 1s.
Broken Wings. With Six Illustrations by W. J. HENNESSY. Crown 8vo, cloth extra, 6s.

MacColl (Hugh), Novels by.
Mr. Stranger's Sealed Packet. Post 8vo, illustrated boards, 2s.
Ednor Whitlock. Crown 8vo, cloth extra, 6s.

Macdonell (Agnes).—Quaker Cousins. Post 8vo, boards, 2s.

MacGregor (Robert).—Pastimes and Players: Notes on Popular Games. Post 8vo, cloth limp, 2s. 6d.

Mackay (Charles, LL.D.). — Interludes and Undertones; or, Music at Twilight. Crown 8vo, cloth extra, 6s.

McCarthy (Justin, M.P.), Works by.

A History of Our Own Times, from the Accession of Queen Victoria to the General Election of 1880. Four Vols., demy 8vo, cloth extra, 12s. each.—Also a POPULAR EDITION, in Four Vols., crown 8vo, cloth extra, 6s. each.—And the JUBILEE EDITION, with an Appendix of Events to the end of 1886, in Two Vols., large crown 8vo, cloth extra, 7s. 6d. each.

A Short History of Our Own Times. One Vol., crown 8vo, cloth extra, 6s.—Also a CHEAP POPULAR EDITION, post 8vo, cloth limp, 2s. 6d.

A History of the Four Georges. Four Vols., demy 8vo, cl. ex., 12s. each. [Vols. I. & II. *ready*

Crown 8vo, cloth extra, 3s. 6d. each; post 8vo, illustrated boards, 2s. each; cloth limp, 2s. 6d. each.

The Waterdale Neighbours.	Donna Quixote. With 12 Illustrations.
My Enemy's Daughter.	The Comet of a Season.
A Fair Saxon.	Maid of Athens. With 12 Illustrations.
Linley Rochford.	Camiola: A Girl with a Fortune.
Dear Lady Disdain.	The Dictator.
Miss Misanthrope. With 12 Illustrations.	Red Diamonds.

'The Right Honourable.' By JUSTIN McCARTHY, M.P., and Mrs. CAMPBELL PRAED. Crown 8vo, cloth extra, 6s.

McCarthy (Justin Huntly), Works by.

The French Revolution. (Constituent Assembly, 1789-91.) Four Vols., demy 8vo, cloth extra, 12s. each. Vols. I. & II. *ready :* Vols. III. & IV. *in the press*

An Outline of the History of Ireland. Crown 8vo, 1s.; cloth, 1s. 6d.

Ireland Since the Union : Sketches of Irish History, 1798-1886. Crown 8vo, cloth, 6s.

Hafiz in London : Poems. Small 8vo, gold cloth, 3s. 6d.

Our Sensation Novel. Crown 8vo, picture cover, 1s.; cloth limp, 1s. 6d.

Doom : An Atlantic Episode. Crown 8vo, picture cover, 1s.

Dolly : A Sketch. Crown 8vo, picture cover, 1s.; cloth limp, 1s. 6d.

Lily Lass : A Romance. Crown 8vo, picture cover, 1s.; cloth limp, 1s. 6d.

The Thousand and One Days. With Two Photogravures. Two Vols., crown 8vo, half-bd., 12s.

A London Legend. Crown 8vo, cloth, 3s. 6d.

MacDonald (George, LL.D.), Books by.

Works of Fancy and Imagination. Ten Vols., 16mo, cloth, gilt edges, in cloth case, 21s.; or the Volumes may be had separately, in Grolier cloth, at 2s. 6d. each.

Vol. I. WITHIN AND WITHOUT.—THE HIDDEN LIFE.
" II. THE DISCIPLE.—THE GOSPEL WOMEN.—BOOK OF SONNETS.—ORGAN SONGS.
" III. VIOLIN SONGS.—SONGS OF THE DAYS AND NIGHTS.—A BOOK OF DREAMS.—ROADSIDE POEMS.—POEMS FOR CHILDREN.
" IV. PARABLES.—BALLADS.—SCOTCH SONGS.
" V. & VI. PHANTASTES: A Faerie Romance. | Vol VII. THE PORTENT.
" VIII. THE LIGHT PRINCESS.—THE GIANT'S HEART.—SHADOWS.
" IX. CROSS PURPOSES.—THE GOLDEN KEY.—THE CARASOYN.—LITTLE DAYLIGHT.
" X. THE CRUEL PAINTER.—THE WOW O' RIVVEN.—THE CASTLE.—THE BROKEN SWORDS.—THE GRAY WOLF.—UNCLE CORNELIUS.

Poetical Works of George MacDonald. Collected and Arranged by the Author. Two Vols. crown 8vo, buckram, 12s.

A Threefold Cord. Edited by GEORGE MACDONALD. Post 8vo, cloth, 5s.

Phantastes : A Faerie Romance. With 25 Illustrations by J. BELL. Crown 8vo, cloth extra, 3s. 6d.

Heather and Snow : A Novel. Crown 8vo, cloth extra, 3s. 6d.; post 8vo, illustrated boards, 2s.

Lilith : A Romance. SECOND EDITION. Crown 8vo, cloth extra, 6s.

Maclise Portrait Gallery (The) of Illustrious Literary Characters: 85 Portraits by DANIEL MACLISE; with Memoirs—Biographical, Critical, Bibliographical, and Anecdotal—illustrative of the Literature of the former half of the Present Century, by WILLIAM BATES, B.A. Crown 8vo, cloth extra, 7s. 6d.

Macquoid (Mrs.), Works by. Square 8vo, cloth extra, 6s. each.

In the Ardennes. With 50 Illustrations by THOMAS R. MACQUOID.

Pictures and Legends from Normandy and Brittany. 34 Illusts. by T. R. MACQUOID.

Through Normandy. With 92 Illustrations by T. R. MACQUOID, and a Map.

Through Brittany. With 35 Illustrations by T. R. MACQUOID, and a Map.

About Yorkshire. With 67 Illustrations by T. R. MACQUOID.

Post 8vo, illustrated boards, 2s. each.

The Evil Eye, and other Stories. | **Lost Rose,** and other Stories.

Magician's Own Book, The: Performances with Eggs, Hats, &c.
Edited by W. H. CREMER. With 200 Illustrations. Crown 8vo; cloth extra, 4s. 6d.

Magic Lantern, The, and its Management: Including full Practical
Directions. By T. C. HEPWORTH. With 10 Illustrations. Crown 8vo, 1s.; cloth, 1s. 6d.

Magna Charta: An Exact Facsimile of the Original in the British
Museum, 3 feet by 2 feet, with Arms and Seals emblazoned in Gold and Colours, 5s.

Mallory (Sir Thomas). — Mort d'Arthur: The Stories of King
Arthur and of the Knights of the Round Table. (A Selection.) Edited by B. MONTGOMERIE RANKING. Post 8vo, cloth limp, 2s.

Mallock (W. H.), Works by.
The New Republic. Post 8vo, picture cover, 2s.; cloth limp, 2s. 6d.
The New Paul & Virginia: Positivism on an Island. Post 8vo, cloth, 2s. 6d.
A Romance of the Nineteenth Century. Crown 8vo, cloth 6s.; pos 8vo, illust. boards, 2s.

Poems. Small 4to, parchment, 8s.
Is Life Worth Living? Crown 8vo, cloth extra, 6s.

Mark Twain, Books by. Crown 8vo, cloth extra, 7s. 6d. each.
The Choice Works of Mark Twain. Revised and Corrected throughout by the Author. With Life, Portrait, and numerous Illustrations.
Roughing It; and The Innocents at Home. With 200 Illustrations by F. A. FRASER.
Mark Twain's Library of Humour. With 197 Illustrations.

Crown 8vo, cloth extra (illustrated), 7s. 6d. each; post 8vo, illustrated boards, 2s. each.
The Innocents Abroad; or, The New Pilgrim's Progress. With 234 Illustrations. (The Two Shilling Edition is entitled Mark Twain's Pleasure Trip.)
The Gilded Age. By MARK TWAIN and C. D. WARNER. With 212 Illustrations.
The Adventures of Tom Sawyer. With 111 Illustrations.
A Tramp Abroad. With 314 Illustrations.
The Prince and the Pauper. With 190 Illustrations.
Life on the Mississippi. With 300 Illustrations.
The Adventures of Huckleberry Finn. With 174 Illustrations by E. W. KEMBLE.
A Yankee at the Court of King Arthur. With 220 Illustrations by DAN BEARD.

Crown 8vo, cloth extra, 3s. 6d. each.
The American Claimant. With 81 Illustrations by HAL HURST and others.
Tom Sawyer Abroad. With 26 Illustrations by DAN. BEARD.
Pudd'nhead Wilson. With Portrait and Six Illustrations by LOUIS LOEB.
Tom Sawyer, Detective, &c. With numerous Illustrations.   [Shortly.

The £1,000,000 Bank-Note. Crown 8vo, cloth, 3s. 6d.; post 8vo, picture boards 2s.

Post 8vo, illustrated boards, 2s. each.
The Stolen White Elephant. | Mark Twain's Sketches.

Marks (H. S., R.A.), Pen and Pencil Sketches by. With Four
Photogravures and 126 Illustrations. Two Vols. demy 8vo, cloth, 32s.

Marlowe's Works. Including his Translations. Edited, with Notes
and Introductions, by Colonel CUNNINGHAM. Crown 8vo, cloth extra, 6s.

Marryat (Florence), Novels by. Post 8vo, illust. boards, 2s. each.
A Harvest of Wild Oats. | Fighting the Air.
Open! Sesame! | Written in Fire.

Massinger's Plays. From the Text of WILLIAM GIFFORD. Edited
by Col. CUNNINGHAM. Crown 8vo, cloth extra, 6s.

Masterman (J.).—Half-a-Dozen Daughters. Post 8vo, boards, 2s.

Matthews (Brander).—A Secret of the Sea, &c. Post 8vo, illus-
trated boards, 2s.; cloth limp, 2s. 6d.

Mayhew (Henry).—London Characters, and the Humorous Side
of London Life. With numerous Illustrations. Crown 8vo, cloth, 3s. 6d.

Meade (L. T.), Novels by.
A Soldier of Fortune. Crown 8vo, cloth, 3s. 6d.; post 8vo, illustrated boards, 2s.
In an Iron Grip. Crown 8vo, cloth, 3s. 6d.
The Voice of the Charmer. Three Vols., 15s. net.

Merrick (Leonard).—The Man who was Good. Post 8vo, illus-
trated boards, 2s.

Mexican Mustang (On a), through Texas to the Rio Grande. By
A. E. SWEET and J. ARMOY KNOX. With 265 Illustrations. Crown 8vo, cloth extra, 7s. 6d.

Middlemass (Jean), Novels by. Post 8vo, illust. boards, 2s. each.
Touch and Go. | Mr. Dorillion.

Miller (Mrs. F. Fenwick).—Physiology for the Young; or, The
House of Life. With numerous Illustrations. Post 8vo, cloth limp, 2s. 6d.

Milton (J. L.), Works by. Post 8vo, 1s. each; cloth, 1s. 6d. each.
The Hygiene of the Skin. With Directions for Diet, Soaps, Baths, Wines, &c.
The Bath in Diseases of the Skin.
The Laws of Life, and their Relation to Diseases of the Skin.

Minto (Wm.).—Was She Good or Bad? Cr. 8vo, 1s.; cloth. 1s. 6d.

Mitford (Bertram), Novels by. Crown 8vo, cloth extra, 3s. 6d. each.
The Gun-Runner: A Romance of Zululand. With a Frontispiece by STANLEY L. WOOD.
The Luck of Gerard Ridgeley. With a Frontispiece by STANLEY L. WOOD.
The King's Assegai. With Six full-page Illustrations by STANLEY L. WOOD.
Renshaw Fanning's Quest. With a Frontispiece by STANLEY L. WOOD.

Molesworth (Mrs.), Novels by.
Hathercourt Rectory. Post 8vo, illustrated boards, 2s.
That Girl in Black. Crown 8vo, cloth, 1s. 6d.

Moncrieff (W. D. Scott=).—The Abdication: An Historical Drama.
With Seven Etchings by JOHN PETTIE, W. Q. ORCHARDSON, J. MACWHIRTER, COLIN HUNTER, R. MACBETH and TOM GRAHAM. Imperial 4to, buckram, 21s.

Moore (Thomas), Works by.
The Epicurean; and Alciphron. Post 8vo, half-bound, 2s.
Prose and Verse; including Suppressed Passages from the MEMOIRS OF LORD BYRON. Edited by R. H. SHEPHERD. With Portrait. Crown 8vo, cloth extra, 7s. 6d.

Muddock (J. E.) Stories by.
Stories Weird and Wonderful. Post 8vo, illustrated boards, 2s.; cloth, 2s. 6d.
The Dead Man's Secret. With Frontispiece by F. BARNARD. Post 8vo, picture boards, 2s.
From the Bosom of the Deep. Post 8vo, illustrated boards, 2s.
Maid Marian and Robin Hood. With 12 Illusts. by STANLEY WOOD. Cr. 8vo, cloth extra, 3s. 6d.
Basile the Jester. With Frontispiece by STANLEY WOOD. Crown 8vo, cloth, 3s. 6d.

Murray (D. Christie), Novels by.
Crown 8vo, cloth extra, 3s. 6d. each; post 8vo, illustrated boards, 2s. each.

A Life's Atonement.	A Model Father.	First Person Singular.
Joseph's Coat. 12 Illusts.	Old Blazer's Hero.	Bob Martin's Little Girl.
Coals of Fire. 3 Illusts.	Cynic Fortune. Frontisp.	Time's Revenges.
Val Strange.	By the Gate of the Sea.	A Wasted Crime.
Hearts.	A Bit of Human Nature.	In Direst Peril.
The Way of the World.		

Mount Despair, &c. With Frontispiece by GRENVILLE MANTON. Crown 8vo, cloth, 3s. 6d.
The Making of a Novelist: An Experiment in Autobiography. With a Collotype Portrait and Vignette. Crown 8vo, art linen, 6s.

Murray (D. Christie) and Henry Herman, Novels by.
Crown 8vo, cloth extra, 3s. 6d. each; post 8vo, illustrated boards, 2s. each.
One Traveller Returns. | **The Bishops' Bible.**
Paul Jones's Alias, &c. With Illustrations by A. FORESTIER and G. NICOLET.

Murray (Henry), Novels by.
Post 8vo, illustrated boards, 2s. each; cloth, 2s. 6d. each.
A Game of Bluff. | **A Song of Sixpence.**

Newbolt (Henry).—Taken from the Enemy. Fcp. 8vo, cloth, 1s. 6d.

Nisbet (Hume), Books by.
'Bail Up.' Crown 8vo, cloth extra, 3s. 6d.; post 8vo, illustrated boards, 2s.
Dr. Bernard St. Vincent. Post 8vo, illustrated boards, 2s.

Lessons in Art. With 21 Illustrations. Crown 8vo, cloth extra, 2s. 6d.
Where Art Begins. With 27 Illustrations. Square 8vo, cloth extra, 7s. 6d.

Norris (W. E.), Novels by. Crown 8vo, cloth, 3s. 6d. each.
Saint Ann's. | **Billy Bellew.** With Frontispiece.   [Shortly.

O'Hanlon (Alice), Novels by. Post 8vo, illustrated boards, 2s. each.
The Unforeseen. | **Chance? or Fate?**

Ouida, Novels by. Cr. 8vo, cl., 3s. 6d. ea.; post 8vo, illust. bds., 2s. ea.

Held in Bondage.	Folle-Farine.	Moths.	Pipistrello.
Tricotrin.	A Dog of Flanders.	In Maremma.	Wanda.
Strathmore.	Pascarel.	Signa.	Bimbi.	Syrlin.
Chandos.	Two Wooden Shoes.	Frescoes.	Othmar.
Cecil Castlemaine's Gage	In a Winter City.	Princess Napraxine.
Under Two Flags.	Ariadne.	Friendship.	Guilderoy.	Ruffino.
Puck.	Idalia.	A Village Commune.	Two Offenders.

Square 8vo, cloth extra, 5s. each.
Bimbi. With Nine Illustrations by EDMUND H. GARRETT.
A Dog of Flanders, &c. With Six Illustrations by EDMUND H. GARRETT.

Santa Barbara, &c. Square 8vo, cloth, 6s.; crown 8vo, cloth, 3s. 6d.; post 8vo, illustrated boards, 2s.
Under Two Flags. POPULAR EDITION. Medium 8vo, 6d.; cloth, 1s.   [Shortly.

Wisdom, Wit, and Pathos, selected from the Works of OUIDA by F. SYDNEY MORRIS. Post 8vo, cloth extra, 5s.—CHEAP EDITION, illustrated boards, 2s.

Ohnet (Georges), Novels by. Post 8vo, illustrated boards, 2s. each.
Doctor Rameau. | A Last Love.
A Weird Gift. Crown 8vo, cloth, 3s. 6d.; post 8vo, picture boards, 2s.

Oliphant (Mrs.), Novels by. Post 8vo, illustrated boards, 2s. each.
The Primrose Path. | Whiteladies.
The Greatest Heiress in England.

O'Reilly (Mrs.).—Phœbe's Fortunes. Post 8vo, illust. boards, 2s.

Page (H. A.), Works by.
Thoreau: His Life and Aims. With Portrait. Post 8vo, cloth limp, 2s. 6d.
Animal Anecdotes. Arranged on a New Principle. Crown 8vo, cloth extra, 5s.

Pandurang Hari; or, Memoirs of a Hindoo. With Preface by Sir
BARTLE FRERE. Crown 8vo, cloth, 3s. 6d.; post 8vo, illustrated boards, 2s.

Pascal's Provincial Letters. A New Translation, with Historical
Introduction and Notes by T. M'CRIE, D.D. Post 8vo, cloth limp, 2s.

Paul (Margaret A.).—Gentle and Simple. Crown 8vo, cloth, with
Frontispiece by HELEN PATERSON, 3s. 6d.; post 8vo, illustrated boards, 2s.

Payn (James), Novels by.
Crown 8vo, cloth extra, 3s. 6d. each; post 8vo, illustrated boards, 2s. each.
Lost Sir Massingberd. | Holiday Tasks.
Walter's Word. | The Canon's Ward. With Portrait.
Less Black than We're Painted. | The Talk of the Town. With 12 Illusts.
By Proxy. | For Cash Only. | Glow-Worm Tales.
High Spirits. | The Mystery of Mirbridge.
Under One Roof. | The Word and the Will.
A Confidential Agent. With 12 Illusts. | The Burnt Million.
A Grape from a Thorn. With 12 Illusts. | Sunny Stories. | A Trying Patient.

Post 8vo, illustrated boards, 2s. each.
Humorous Stories. | From Exile. | Found Dead.
The Foster Brothers. | Gwendoline's Harvest.
The Family Scapegrace. | A Marine Residence.
Married Beneath Him. | Mirk Abbey.
Bentinck's Tutor. | Some Private Views.
A Perfect Treasure. | Not Wooed, But Won.
A County Family. | Two Hundred Pounds Reward.
Like Father, Like Son. | The Best of Husbands.
A Woman's Vengeance. | Halves.
Carlyon's Year. | Cecil's Tryst. | Fallen Fortunes.
Murphy's Master. | What He Cost Her.
At Her Mercy. | Kit: A Memory.
The Clyffards of Clyffe. | A Prince of the Blood.

In Peril and Privation. With 17 Illustrations. Crown 8vo, cloth, 3s. 6d.
Notes from the 'News.' Crown 8vo, portrait cover, 1s.; cloth, 1s. 6d.

Pennell (H. Cholmondeley), Works by. Post 8vo, cloth, 2s. 6d. ea.
Puck on Pegasus. With Illustrations.
Pegasus Re-Saddled. With Ten full-page Illustrations by G. DU MAURIER.
The Muses of Mayfair: Vers de Société. Selected by H. C. PENNELL.

Phelps (E. Stuart), Works by. Post 8vo, 1s. ea.; cloth, 1s. 6d. ea.
Beyond the Gates. | An Old Maid's Paradise. | Burglars in Paradise.
Jack the Fisherman. Illustrated by C. W. REED. Crown 8vo, 1s.; cloth, 1s. 6d.

Phil May's Sketch-Book. Containing 50 full-page Drawings. Imp.
4to, art canvas, gilt top, 10s. 6d.

Pirkis (C. L.), Novels by.
Trooping with Crows. Fcap. 8vo, picture cover, 1s.
Lady Lovelace. Post 8vo, illustrated boards, 2s.

Planche (J. R.), Works by.
The Pursuivant of Arms. With Six Plates and 209 Illustrations. Crown 8vo, cloth, 7s. 6d.
Songs and Poems, 1819-1879. With Introduction by Mrs. MACKARNESS. Crown 8vo, cloth, 6s.

Plutarch's Lives of Illustrious Men. With Notes and a Life of
Plutarch by JOHN and WM. LANGHORNE, and Portraits. Two Vols., demy 8vo, half-bound 10s. 6d.

Poe's (Edgar Allan) Choice Works in Prose and Poetry. With Introduction by CHARLES BAUDELAIRE. Portrait and Facsimiles. Crown 8vo, cloth, 7s. 6d.
The Mystery of Marie Roget, &c. Post 8vo, illustrated boards, 2s.

Pope's Poetical Works. Post 8vo, cloth limp, 2s.

Praed (Mrs. Campbell), Novels by. Post 8vo, illust. bds., 2s. each.
The Romance of a Station. | The Soul of Countess Adrian.
Crown 8vo, cloth, 3s. 6d. each · post 8vo, boards, 2s. each.
Outlaw and Lawmaker. | Christina Chard. With Frontispiece by W. PAGET.
Mrs. Tregaskiss. Three Vols., crown 8vo, 15s. net.

Price (E. C.), Novels by.
Crown 8vo, cloth extra, 3s. 6d. each; post 8vo, illustrated boards, 2s. each.
Valentina. | The Foreigners. | Mrs. Lancaster's Rival.
Gerald. Post 8vo, illustrated boards, 2s.

Princess Olga.—Radna: A Novel. Crown 8vo, cloth extra, 6s.

Proctor (Richard A., B.A.), Works by.
Flowers of the Sky. With 55 Illustrations. Small crown 8vo, cloth extra, 3s. 6d.
Easy Star Lessons. With Star Maps for every Night in the Year. Crown 8vo, cloth, 6s.
Familiar Science Studies. Crown 8vo, cloth extra, 6s.
Saturn and its System. With 13 Steel Plates. Demy 8vo, cloth extra, 10s. 6d.
Mysteries of Time and Space. With numerous Illustrations. Crown 8vo, cloth extra, 6s.
The Universe of Suns, &c. With numerou; Illustrations. Crown 8vo, cloth extra, 6s.
Wages and Wants of Science Workers. Crown 8vo, 1s. 6d.

Pryce (Richard).—Miss Maxwell's Affections. Crown 8vo, cloth.
with Frontispiece by HAL LUDLOW, 3s. 6d.; post 8vo, illustrated boards, 2s.

Rambosson (J.).—Popular Astronomy. Translated by C. B. PIT-
MAN. With Coloured Frontispiece and numerous Illustrations. Crown 8vo, cloth extra, 7s. 6d.

Randolph (Lieut.-Col. George, U.S.A.).—Aunt Abigail Dykes:
A Novel. Crown 8vo, cloth extra, 7s. 6d.

Reade's (Charles) Novels.
Crown 8vo, cloth extra, mostly Illustrated, 3s. 6d. each; post 8vo, illustrated boards, 2s. each.

Peg Woffington. | Christie Johnstone.
'It is Never Too Late to Mend.'
The Course of True Love Never Did Run
Smooth.
The Autobiography of a Thief; Jack of
all Trades; and James Lambert.
Love Me Little, Love Me Long.
The Double Marriage.
The Cloister and the Hearth.

Hard Cash. | Griffith Gaunt.
Foul Play. | Put Yourself in His Place.
A Terrible Temptation.
A Simpleton. | The Wandering Heir.
A Woman-Hater.
Singleheart and Doubleface.
Good Stories of Men and other Animals.
The Jilt, and other Stories.
A Perilous Secret. | Readiana.

A New Collected LIBRARY EDITION, complete in Seventeen Volumes, set in new long primer type,
printed on laid paper, and elegantly bound in cloth, price 3s. 6d. each, is now in course of publication. The
volumes will appear in the following order:—

1. Peg Woffington; and Christie Johnstone.
2. Hard Cash.
3. The Cloister and the Hearth. With a
Preface by Sir WALTER BESANT.
4. 'It is Never too Late to Mend.'
5. The Course of True Love Never Did
Run Smooth; and Singleheart and
Doubleface.
6. The Autobiography of a Thief; Jack
of all Trades; A Hero and a Mar-
tyr; and The Wandering Heir.

7. Love Me Little, Love me Long.
8. The Double Marriage. [April.
9. Griffith Gaunt. [May.
10. Foul Play. [June.
11. Put Yourself in His Place. [July.
12. A Terrible Temptation. [August.
13. A Simpleton. [Sept.
14. A Woman-Hater. [Oct.
15. The Jilt, and other Stories; and Good
Stories of Men & other Animals.[Nov.
16. A Perilous Secret. [Dec.
17. Readiana; & Bible Characters.[Jan.'97

POPULAR EDITIONS, medium 8vo, 6d. each: cloth, 1s. each.
'It is Never Too Late to Mend.' | The Cloister and the Hearth.
Peg Woffington; and Christie Johnstone.

'It is Never Too Late to Mend' and The Cloister and the Hearth in One Volume,
medium 8vo, cloth, 2s.

Christie Johnstone. With Frontispiece. Choicely printed in Elzevir style. Fcap. 8vo, half-Roxb.2s.6d.
Peg Woffington. Choicely printed in Elzevir style. Fcap. 8vo, half-Roxburghe, 2s. 6d.
The Cloister and the Hearth. In Four Vols., post 8vo, with an Introduction by Sir WALTER BE-
SANT, and a Frontispiece to each Vol., 14s. the set; and the ILLUSTRATED LIBRARY EDITION,
with Illustrations on every page, Two Vols., crown 8vo, cloth gilt, 42s. net.
Bible Characters. Fcap. 8vo, leatherette, 1s.

Selections from the Works of Charles Reade. With an Introduction by Mrs. ALEX. IRE-
LAND. Crown 8vo, buckram, with Portrait, 6s.; CHEAP EDITION, post 8vo, cloth limp, 2s. 6d.

Riddell (Mrs. J. H.), Novels by.
Weird Stories. Crown 8vo, cloth extra, 3s. 6d.; post 8vo, illustrated boards, 2s.

Post 8vo, illustrated boards, 2s. each.
The Uninhabited House.
The Prince of Wales's Garden Party.
The Mystery in Palace Gardens.

Fairy Water.
Her Mother's Darling.
The Nun's Curse. | Idle Tales.

Rimmer (Alfred), Works by. Square 8vo, cloth gilt, 7s. 6d. each.
Our Old Country Towns. With 55 Illustrations by the Author.
Rambles Round Eton and Harrow. With 50 Illustrations by the Author.
About England with Dickens. With 58 Illustrations by C. A. VANDERHOOF and A. RIMMER.

Rives (Amelie).—Barbara Dering. Crown 8vo, cloth extra, 3s. 6d. ;
post 8vo, illustrated boards, 2s.

Robinson Crusoe. By DANIEL DEFOE. With 37 Illustrations by
GEORGE CRUIKSHANK. Post 8vo, half-cloth, 2s. ; cloth extra, gilt edges, 2s. 6d.

Robinson (F. W.), Novels by.
Women are Strange. Post 8vo, illustrated boards, 2s.
The Hands of Justice. Crown 8vo, cloth extra, 3s. 6d. ; post 8vo, illustrated boards, 2s.

The Woman in the Dark. Two Vols., 10s. net.

Robinson (Phil), Works by. Crown 8vo, cloth extra, 6s. each.
The Poets' Birds. | **The Poets' Beasts.**
The Poets and Nature: Reptiles, Fishes, and Insects.

Rochefoucauld's Maxims and Moral Reflections. With Notes
and an Introductory Essay by SAINTE-BEUVE. Post 8vo, cloth limp, 2s.

Roll of Battle Abbey, The: A List of the Principal Warriors who
came from Normandy with William the Conqueror, 1066. Printed in Gold and Colours, 5s.

Rosengarten (A.).—A Handbook of Architectural Styles. Translated by W. COLLETT-SANDARS. With 630 Illustrations. Crown 8vo, cloth extra, 7s. 6d.

Rowley (Hon. Hugh), Works by. Post 8vo, cloth, 2s. 6d. each.
Puniana: Riddles and Jokes. With numerous Illustrations.
More Puniana. Profusely Illustrated.

Runciman (James), Stories by. Post 8vo, bds., 2s. ea.; cl., 2s. 6d. ea.
Skippers and Shellbacks. | **Grace Balmaign's Sweetheart.**
Schools and Scholars.

Russell (Dora), Novels by. Crown 8vo, cloth, 3s. 6d. each.
A Country Sweetheart. | **The Drift of Fate.**   [Shortly.

Russell (W. Clark), Books and Novels by.
Crown 8vo, cloth extra, 6s. each ; post 8vo, illustrated boards, 2s. each ; cloth limp, 2s. 6d. each.
Round the Galley-Fire. | **A Book for the Hammock.**
In the Middle Watch. | **The Mystery of the 'Ocean Star.'**
A Voyage to the Cape. | **The Romance of Jenny Harlowe.**

Crown 8vo, cloth extra, 3s. 6d. each ; post 8vo, illustrated boards, 2s. each ; cloth limp, 2s. 6d. each.
An Ocean Tragedy. | **My Shipmate Louise.** | **Alone on a Wide Wide Sea.**

Crown 8vo, cloth, 3s. 6d. each.
Is He the Man? | **The Phantom Death, &c.** With Frontispiece.
The Good Ship 'Mohock.' | **The Convict Ship.**   [Shortly.

On the Fo'k'sle Head. Post 8vo, illustrated boards, 2s. ; cloth limp, 2s. 6d.
Heart of Oak. Three Vols., crown 8vo, 15s. net.
The Tale of the Ten. Three Vols., crown 8vo, 15s. net.

Saint Aubyn (Alan), Novels by.
Crown 8vo, cloth extra, 3s. 6d. each ; post 8vo, illustrated boards, 2s. each.
A Fellow of Trinity. With a Note by OLIVER WENDELL HOLMES and a Frontispiece.
The Junior Dean. | **The Master of St. Benedict's.** | **To His Own Master.**
                                    Orchard Damerel.

Fcap. 8vo, cloth boards, 1s. 6d. each.
The Old Maid's Sweetheart. | **Modest Little Sara.**

Crown 8vo, cloth extra, 3s. 6d. each.
In the Face of the World. | **The Tremlett Diamonds.**   [Shortly.

Sala (George A.).—Gaslight and Daylight. Post 8vo, boards, 2s.

Sanson. — Seven Generations of Executioners: Memoirs of the
Sanson Family (1688 to 1847). Crown 8vo, cloth extra, 3s. 6d.

Saunders (John), Novels by.
Crown 8vo, cloth extra, 3s. 6d. each ; post 8vo, illustrated boards, 2s. each.
Guy Waterman. | **The Lion in the Path.** | **The Two Dreamers.**
Bound to the Wheel. Crown 8vo, cloth extra, 3s. 6d.

Saunders (Katharine), Novels by.
Crown 8vo, cloth extra, 3s. 6d. each ; post 8vo, illustrated boards, 2s. each.

| **Margaret and Elizabeth.** | **Heart Salvage.** |
| **The High Mills.** | **Sebastian.** |

Joan Merryweather. Post 8vo, illustrated boards, 2s.
Gideon's Rock. Crown 8vo, cloth extra, 3s. 6d.

Scotland Yard, Past and Present: Experiences of Thirty-seven Years.
By Ex-Chief-Inspector CAVANAGH. Post 8vo, illustrated boards, 2s. ; cloth, 2s. 6d.

Secret Out, The: One Thousand Tricks with Cards; with Entertaining Experiments in Drawing-room or 'White' Magic. By W. H. CREMER. With 300 Illustrations. Crown 8vo, cloth extra, 4s. 6d.

Seguin (L. G.), Works by.
The Country of the Passion Play (Oberammergau) and the Highlands of Bavaria. With Map and 37 Illustrations. Crown 8vo, cloth extra, 3s. 6d.
Walks in Algiers. With Two Maps and 16 Illustrations. Crown 8vo, cloth extra, 6s.

Senior (Wm.).—By Stream and Sea. Post 8vo, cloth, 2s. 6d.

Sergeant (Adeline).—Dr. Endicott's Experiment. Crown 8vo, buckram, 3s. 6d.

Shakespeare for Children: Lamb's Tales from Shakespeare.
With Illustrations, coloured and plain, by J. MOYR SMITH. Crown 4to, cloth gilt, 3s. 6d.

Sharp (William).—Children of To-morrow. Crown 8vo, cloth, 6s.

Shelley's (Percy Bysshe) Complete Works in Verse and Prose.
Edited, Prefaced, and Annotated by R. HERNE SHEPHERD. Five Vols., crown 8vo, cloth, 3s. 6d. each.
Poetical Works, in Three Vols.:
Vol. I. Introduction by the Editor: Posthumous Fragments of Margaret Nicholson; Shelley's Correspondence with Stockdale; The Wandering Jew; Queen Mab, with the Notes; Alastor, and other Poems; Rosalind and Helen; Prometheus Unbound; Adonais, &c.
  II. Laon and Cythna: The Cenci; Julian and Maddalo; Swellfoot the Tyrant; The Witch of Atlas; Epipsychidion; Hellas.
 ,, III. Posthumous Poems; The Masque of Anarchy; and other Pieces.
Prose Works, in Two Vols.:
Vol. I. The Two Romances of Zastrozzi and St. Irvyne: the Dublin and Marlow Pamphlets; A Refutation of Deism; Letters to Leigh Hunt, and some Minor Writings and Fragments.
 ,, II. The Essays; Letters from Abroad; Translations and Fragments, edited by Mrs. SHELLEY. With a Biography of Shelley, and an Index of the Prose Works.
⁎ Also a few copies of a LARGE-PAPER EDITION, 5 vols., cloth, £2 12s. 6d.

Sherard (R. H.).—Rogues: A Novel. Crown 8vo, 1s. ; cloth, 1s. 6d.

Sheridan (General P. H.), Personal Memoirs of. With Portraits,
Maps, and Facsimiles. Two Vols., demy 8vo, cloth, 24s.

Sheridan's (Richard Brinsley) Complete Works, with Life and
Anecdotes. Including his Dramatic Writings, his Works in Prose and Poetry, Translations, Speeches, and Jokes. With 10 Illustrations. Crown 8vo, half-bound, 7s. 6d.
The Rivals, The School for Scandal, and other Plays. Post 8vo, half-bound, 2s.
Sheridan's Comedies: The Rivals and **The School for Scandal.** Edited, with an Introduction and Notes to each Play, and a Biographical Sketch, by BRANDER MATTHEWS. With Illustrations. Demy 8vo, half-parchment, 12s. 6d.

Sidney's (Sir Philip) Complete Poetical Works, including all
those in 'Arcadia.' With Portrait, Memorial-Introduction, Notes, &c., by the Rev. A. B. GROSART, D.D. Three Vols., crown 8vo, cloth boards, 18s.

Sims (George R.), Works by.
Post 8vo, illustrated boards, 2s. each ; cloth limp, 2s. 6d. each.

Rogues and Vagabonds.	**Tales of To-day.**
The Ring o' Bells.	**Dramas of Life.** With 60 Illustrations.
Mary Jane's Memoirs.	**Memoirs of a Landlady.**
Mary Jane Married.	**My Two Wives.**
Tinkletop's Crime.	**Scenes from the Show.**
Zeph: A Circus Story, &c.	**The Ten Commandments:** Stories. [Shortly.

Crown 8vo, picture cover, 1s. each ; cloth, 1s. 6d. each.
How the Poor Live; and Horrible London.
The Dagonet Reciter and Reader: Being Readings and Recitations in Prose and Verse, selected from his own Works by GEORGE R. SIMS.
The Case of George Candlemas. | **Dagonet Ditties.** (From The Referee.)

Dagonet Abroad. Crown 8vo, cloth, 3s. 6d.

Signboards: Their History, including Anecdotes of Famous Taverns and Remarkable Characters. By JACOB LARWOOD and JOHN CAMDEN HOTTEN. With Coloured Frontispiece and 94 Illustrations. Crown 8vo, cloth extra, 7s. 6d.

Sister Dora: A Biography. By MARGARET LONSDALE. With Four Illustrations. Demy 8vo, picture cover, 4d.; cloth, 6d.

Sketchley (Arthur).—A Match in the Dark. Post 8vo, boards, 2s.

Slang Dictionary (The): Etymological, Historical, and Anecdotal. Crown 8vo, cloth extra, 6s. 6d.

Smart (Hawley).—Without Love or Licence: A Novel. Crown 8vo, cloth extra, 3s. 6d.; post 8vo, illustrated boards, 2s.

Smith (J. Moyr), Works by.
The Prince of Argolis. With 130 Illustrations. Post 8vo, cloth extra, 3s. 6d.
The Wooing of the Water Witch. With numerous Illustrations. Post 8vo, cloth, 6s.

Society in London. Crown 8vo, 1s.; cloth, 1s. 6d.

Society in Paris: The Upper Ten Thousand. A Series of Letters from Count PAUL VASILI to a Young French Diplomat. Crown 8vo, cloth, 6s.

Somerset (Lord Henry).—Songs of Adieu. Small 4to, Jap. vel., 6s.

Spalding (T. A., LL.B.).— Elizabethan Demonology: An Essay on the Belief in the Existence of Devils. Crown 8vo, cloth extra, 5s.

Speight (T. W.), Novels by.
Post 8vo, illustrated boards, 2s. each.

The Mysteries of Heron Dyke.	Back to Life.
By Devious Ways, &c.	The Loudwater Tragedy.
Hoodwinked; & Sandycroft Mystery.	Burgo's Romance.
The Golden Hoop.	Quittance in Full.

Post 8vo, cloth limp, 1s. 6d. each.

A Barren Title.	Wife or No Wife?

Crown 8vo, cloth extra, 3s. 6d. each.

A Secret of the Sea.	The Grey Monk.

The Sandycroft Mystery. Crown 8vo, picture cover, 1s.
The Master of Trenance. Three Vols., crown 8vo, 15s. net.
A Husband from the Sea. Post 8vo, illustrated boards, 2s.

Spenser for Children. By M. H. TOWRY. With Coloured Illustrations by WALTER J. MORGAN. Crown 4to, cloth extra, 3s. 6d.

Stafford (John).—Doris and I, &c. Crown 8vo, cloth, 3s. 6d. [Shortly.

Starry Heavens (The): A POETICAL BIRTHDAY BOOK. Royal 16mo, cloth extra, 2s. 6d.

Stedman (E. C.), Works by. Crown 8vo, cloth extra, 9s. each.
Victorian Poets. | The Poets of America.

Stephens (Riccardo, M.B.).—The Cruciform Mark: The Strange Story of RICHARD TREGENNA, Bachelor of Medicine (Univ. Edinb.) Crown 8vo, cloth, 6s.

Sterndale (R. Armitage).—The Afghan Knife: A Novel. Crown 8vo, cloth extra, 3s. 6d.; post 8vo, illustrated boards, 2s.

Stevenson (R. Louis), Works by. Post 8vo, cloth limp, 2s. 6d. ea.
Travels with a Donkey. With a Frontispiece by WALTER CRANE.
An Inland Voyage. With a Frontispiece by WALTER CRANE.

Crown 8vo, buckram, gilt top, 6s. each.
Familiar Studies of Men and Books.
The Silverado Squatters. With Frontispiece by J. D. STRONG.
The Merry Men. | Underwoods: Poems.
Memories and Portraits.
Virginibus Puerisque, and other Papers. | Ballads. | Prince Otto.
Across the Plains, with other Memories and Essays.

New Arabian Nights. Crown 8vo, buckram, gilt top, 6s.; post 8vo, illustrated boards, 2s.
The Suicide Club; and The Rajah's Diamond. (From NEW ARABIAN NIGHTS.) With Eight Illustrations by W. J. HENNESSY. Crown 8vo, cloth, 5s.
The Edinburgh Edition of the Works of Robert Louis Stevenson. Twenty-seven Vols., demy 8vo. This Edition (which is limited to 1,000 copies) is sold only in Sets, the price of which may be learned from the Booksellers. The First Volume was published Nov., 1894.

Songs of Travel. Crown 8vo, buckram, 5s. [Shortly.
Weir of Hermiston. (R. L. STEVENSON'S LAST WORK.) Large crown 8vo, 6s. [May.

Stoddard (C. Warren).—Summer Cruising in the South Seas.
Illustrated by WALLIS MACKAY. Crown 8vo, cloth extra, 3s. 6d.

Stories from Foreign Novelists. With Notices by HELEN and
ALICE ZIMMERN. Crown 8vo, cloth extra, 3s. 6d.; post 8vo, illustrated boards, 2s.

Strange Manuscript (A) Found in a Copper Cylinder. Crown
8vo, cloth extra, with 19 Illustrations by GILBERT GAUL, 5s.; post 8vo, illustrated boards, 2s.

Strange Secrets. Told by PERCY FITZGERALD, CONAN DOYLE, FLOR-
ENCE MARRYAT, &c. Post 8vo, illustrated boards, 2s.

**Strutt (Joseph). — The Sports and Pastimes of the People of
England;** including the Rural and Domestic Recreations, May Games, Mummeries, Shows, &c., from
the Earliest Period to the Present Time. Edited by WILLIAM HONE. With 140 Illustrations. Crown
8vo, cloth extra, 7s. 6d.

Swift's (Dean) Choice Works, in Prose and Verse. With Memoir,
Portrait, and Facsimiles of the Maps in 'Gulliver's Travels.' Crown 8vo, cloth, 7s. 6d.
Gulliver's Travels, and **A Tale of a Tub.** Post 8vo, half-bound, 2s.
Jonathan Swift: A Study. By J. CHURTON COLLINS. Crown 8vo, cloth extra, 8s.

Swinburne (Algernon C.), Works by.

Selections from the Poetical Works of
A. C. Swinburne. Fcap. 8vo, 6s.
Atalanta in Calydon. Crown 8vo, 6s.
Chastelard: A Tragedy. Crown 8vo, 7s.
Poems and Ballads. FIRST SERIES. Crown
8vo, or fcap. 8vo, 9s.
Poems and Ballads. SECOND SERIES. Crown
8vo, 9s.
Poems & Ballads. THIRD SERIES. Cr. 8vo, 7s.
Songs before Sunrise. Crown 8vo, 10s. 6d.
Bothwell: A Tragedy. Crown 8vo, 12s. 6d.
Songs of Two Nations. Crown 8vo, 6s.
George Chapman. (See Vol. II. of G. CHAP-
MAN'S Works.) Crown 8vo, 6s.
Essays and Studies. Crown 8vo, 12s.
Erechtheus: A Tragedy. Crown 8vo, 6s.

A Note on Charlotte Bronte. Cr. 8vo, 6s
A Study of Shakespeare. Crown 8vo, 8s.
Songs of the Springtides. Crown 8vo, 6s.
Studies in Song. Crown 8vo, 7s.
Mary Stuart: A Tragedy. Crown 8vo, 8s.
Tristram of Lyonesse. Crown 8vo, 9s.
A Century of Roundels. Small 4to, 8s.
A Midsummer Holiday. Crown 8vo, 7s.
Marino Faliero: A Tragedy. Crown 8vo, 6s.
A Study of Victor Hugo. Crown 8vo, 6s.
Miscellanies. Crown 8vo, 12s.
Locrine: A Tragedy. Crown 8vo, 6s.
A Study of Ben Jonson. Crown 8vo, 7s.
The Sisters: A Tragedy. Crown 8vo, 6s.
Astrophel, &c. Crown 8vo, 7s.
Studies in Prose and Poetry. Cr.8vo, 9s.

Syntax's (Dr.) Three Tours: In Search of the Picturesque, in Search
of Consolation, and in Search of a Wife. With ROWLANDSON'S Coloured Illustrations, and Life of the
Author by J. C. HOTTEN. Crown 8vo, cloth extra, 7s. 6d.

Taine's History of English Literature. Translated by HENRY VAN
LAUN. Four Vols., small demy 8vo, cloth boards, 30s.—POPULAR EDITION, Two Vols., large crown
8vo, cloth extra, 15s.

Taylor (Bayard). — Diversions of the Echo Club: Burlesques of
Modern Writers. Post 8vo, cloth limp, 2s.

Taylor (Dr. J. E., F.L.S.), Works by. Crown 8vo, cloth, 5s. each.
The Sagacity and Morality of Plants: A Sketch of the Life and Conduct of the Vegetable
Kingdom. With a Coloured Frontispiece and 100 Illustrations.
Our Common British Fossils, and Where to Find Them. With 331 Illustrations.
The Playtime Naturalist. With 366 Illustrations.

Taylor (Tom). — Historical Dramas. Containing 'Clancarty,'
'Jeanne Darc,' 'Twixt Axe and Crown,' 'The Fool's Revenge,' 'Arkwright's Wife,' 'Anne Boleyn,'
'Plot and Passion.' Crown 8vo, cloth extra, 7s. 6d.
. The Plays may also be had separately, at 1s. each.

Tennyson (Lord): A Biographical Sketch. By H. J. JENNINGS. Post
8vo, portrait cover, 1s.; cloth, 1s. 6d.

Thackerayana: Notes and Anecdotes. With Coloured Frontispiece and
Hundreds of Sketches by WILLIAM MAKEPEACE THACKERAY. Crown 8vo, cloth extra, 7s. 6d.

Thames, A New Pictorial History of the. By A. S. KRAUSSE.
With 340 Illustrations. Post 8vo, 1s.; cloth, 1s. 6d.

**Thiers (Adolphe). — History of the Consulate and Empire of
France under Napoleon.** Translated by D. FORBES CAMPBELL and JOHN STEBBING. With 36 Steel
Plates. 12 Vols., demy 8vo, cloth extra, 12s. each.

Thomas (Bertha), Novels by. Cr. 8vo, cl., 3s. 6d. ea.; post 8vo, 2s. ea.
The Violin-Player. | Proud Maisie.

Cressida. Post 8vo, illustrated boards, 2s.

Thomson's Seasons, and The Castle of Indolence. With Introduction by ALLAN CUNNINGHAM, and 48 Illustrations. Post 8vo, half-bound, 2s.

Thornbury (Walter), Books by.
The Life and Correspondence of J. M. W. Turner. With Illustrations in Colours. Crown 8vo, cloth extra, 7s. 6d.

Post 8vo, illustrated boards, 2s. each.
Old Stories Re-told. | Tales for the Marines.

Timbs (John), Works by. Crown 8vo, cloth extra, 7s. 6d. each.
The History of Clubs and Club Life in London: Anecdotes of its Famous Coffee-houses, Hostelries, and Taverns. With 42 Illustrations.
English Eccentrics and Eccentricities: Stories of Delusions, Impostures, Sporting Scenes, Eccentric Artists, Theatrical Folk, &c. With 48 Illustrations.

Transvaal (The). By JOHN DE VILLIERS. With Map. Crown 8vo, 1s.

Trollope (Anthony), Novels by.
Crown 8vo, cloth extra, 3s. 6d. each; post 8vo, illustrated boards, 2s. each.
The Way We Live Now. | Mr. Scarborough's Family.
Frau Frohmann. | The Land-Leaguers.

Post 8vo, illustrated boards, 2s. each.
Kept in the Dark. | The American Senator.
The Golden Lion of Granpere. | John Caldigate. | Marion Fay.

Trollope (Frances E.), Novels by.
Crown 8vo, cloth extra, 3s. 6d. each; post 8vo, illustrated boards, 2s. each.
Like Ships Upon the Sea. | Mabel's Progress. | Anne Furness.

Trollope (T. A.).—Diamond Cut Diamond. Post 8vo, illust. bds., 2s.

Trowbridge (J. T.).—Farnell's Folly. Post 8vo, illust. boards, 2s.

Tytler (C. C. Fraser-).—Mistress Judith: A Novel. Crown 8vo, cloth extra, 3s. 6d.; post 8vo, illustrated boards, 2s.

Tytler (Sarah), Novels by.
Crown 8vo, cloth extra, 3s. 6d. each; post 8vo, illustrated boards, 2s. each.
Lady Bell. | Buried Diamonds. | The Blackhall Ghosts.

Post 8vo, illustrated boards, 2s. each.
What She Came Through. | The Huguenot Family.
Citoyenne Jacqueline. | Noblesse Oblige.
The Bride's Pass. | Beauty and the Beast.
Saint Mungo's City. | Disappeared.

The Macdonald Lass. With Frontispiece. Crown 8vo, cloth, 3s. 6d.

Upward (Allen), Novels by.
The Queen Against Owen. Crown 8vo, cloth, with Frontispiece, 3s. 6d.; post 8vo, boards, 2s.
The Prince of Balkistan. Crown 8vo, cloth extra, 3s. 6d.
A Crown of Straw. Crown 8vo, cloth, 6s. [Shortly.

Vashti and Esther. By the Writer of 'Belle's' Letters in The World. Crown 8vo, cloth extra, 3s. 6d.

Villari (Linda).—A Double Bond: A Story. Fcap. 8vo, 1s.

Vizetelly (Ernest A.).—The Scorpion: A Romance of Spain. With a Frontispiece. Crown 8vo, cloth extra, 3s. 6d.

Walton and Cotton's Complete Angler; or, The Contemplative Man's Recreation, by IZAAK WALTON; and Instructions How to Angle, for a Trout or Grayling in a clear Stream, by CHARLES COTTON. With Memoirs and Notes by Sir HARRIS NICOLAS, and 61 Illustrations. Crown 8vo, cloth antique, 7s. 6d.

Walt Whitman, Poems by. Edited, with Introduction, by WILLIAM M. ROSSETTI. With Portrait. Crown 8vo, hand-made paper and buckram, 6s.

Ward (Herbert), Books by.
Five Years with the Congo Cannibals. With 92 Illustrations. Royal 8vo, cloth, 14s.
My Life with Stanley's Rear Guard. With Map. Post 8vo, 1s.; cloth, 1s. 6d.

Walford (Edward, M.A.), Works by.

Walford's County Families of the United Kingdom (1896). Containing the Descent, Birth, Marriage, Education, &c., of 12,000 Heads of Families, their Heirs, Offices, Addresses, Clubs, &c. Royal 8vo, cloth gilt, 50s.

Walford's Shilling Peerage (1896). Containing a List of the House of Lords, Scotch and Irish Peers, &c. 32mo, cloth, 1s.

Walford's Shilling Baronetage (1896). Containing a List of the Baronets of the United Kingdom, Biographical Notices, Addresses, &c. 32mo, cloth, 1s.

Walford's Shilling Knightage (1896). Containing a List of the Knights of the United Kingdom, Biographical Notices, Addresses, &c. 32mo, cloth, 1s.

Walford's Shilling House of Commons (1896). Containing a List of all the Members of the New Parliament, their Addresses, Clubs, &c. 32mo, cloth, 1s.

Walford's Complete Peerage, Baronetage, Knightage, and House of Commons (1896). Royal 32mo, cloth, gilt edges, 5s.

Tales of our Great Families. Crown 8vo, cloth extra, 3s. 6d.

Warner (Charles Dudley).—A Roundabout Journey. Crown 8vo, cloth extra, 6s.

Warrant to Execute Charles I. A Facsimile, with the 59 Signatures and Seals. Printed on paper 22 in. by 14 in. 2s.

Warrant to Execute Mary Queen of Scots. A Facsimile, including Queen Elizabeth's Signature and the Great Seal. 2s.

Washington's (George) Rules of Civility Traced to their Sources and Restored by MONCURE D. CONWAY. Fcap. 8vo, Japanese vellum, 2s. 6d.

Wassermann (Lillias), Novels by.

The Daffodils. Crown 8vo, 1s. ; cloth, 1s. 6d.

The Marquis of Carabas. By AARON WATSON and LILLIAS WASSERMANN. Post 8vo, illustrated boards, 2s.

Weather, How to Foretell the, with the Pocket Spectroscope. By F. W. CORY. With Ten Illustrations. Crown 8vo, 1s. ; cloth, 1s. 6d.

Webber (Byron).—Fun, Frolic, and Fancy. With 43 Illustrations by PHIL MAY and CHARLES MAY. Fcap. 4to, cloth, 5s.

Westall (William), Novels by.

Trust-Money. Post 8vo, illustrated boards, 2s. ; cloth, 2s. 6d.

Sons of Belial. Two Vols., crown 8vo, 10s. net.

Westbury (Atha).—The Shadow of Hilton Fernbrook: A Romance of Maoriland. Crown 8vo, cloth, 3s. 6d.   [Shortly.

Whist, How to Play Solo. By ABRAHAM S. WILKS and CHARLES F. PARDON. Post 8vo, cloth limp, 2s.

White (Gilbert).—The Natural History of Selborne. Post 8vo, printed on laid paper and half-bound, 2s.

Williams (W. Mattieu, F.R.A.S.), Works by.

Science in Short Chapters. Crown 8vo, cloth extra, 7s. 6d.

A Simple Treatise on Heat. With Illustrations. Crown 8vo, cloth, 2s. 6d.

The Chemistry of Cookery. Crown 8vo, cloth extra, 6s.

The Chemistry of Iron and Steel Making. Crown 8vo, cloth extra, 9s.

A Vindication of Phrenology. With Portrait and 43 Illusts. Demy 8vo, cloth extra, 12s. 6d.

Williamson (Mrs. F. H.).—A Child Widow. Post 8vo, bds., 2s.

Wills (W. H., M.D.).—An Easy-going Fellow. Crown 8vo, cloth, 6s.   [Short'y.

Wilson (Dr. Andrew, F.R.S.E.), Works by.

Chapters on Evolution. With 259 Illustrations. Crown 8vo, cloth extra, 7s. 6d.

Leaves from a Naturalist's Note-Book. Post 8vo, cloth limp, 2s. 6d.

Leisure-Time Studies. With Illustrations. Crown 8vo, cloth extra, 6s.

Studies in Life and Sense. With numerous Illustrations. Crown 8vo, cloth extra, 6s.

Common Accidents: How to Treat Them. With Illustrations. Crown 8vo, 1s. ; cloth, 1s. 6d.

Glimpses of Nature. With 35 Illustrations. Crown 8vo, cloth extra, 3s. 6d.

Winter (J. S.), Stories by. Post 8vo, illustrated boards, 2s. each ; cloth limp, 2s. 6d. each.

Cavalry Life. | **Regimental Legends.**

A Soldier's Children. With 34 Illustrations by E. G. THOMSON and E. STUART HARDY. Crown 8vo, cloth extra, 3s. 6d.

Wissmann (Hermann von). — My Second Journey through Equatorial Africa. With 92 Illustrations. Demy 8vo, cloth, 16s.

Wood (H. F.), Detective Stories by. Post 8vo, boards, 2s. each.
The Passenger from Scotland Yard. | The Englishman of the Rue Cain.

Wood (Lady).—Sabina: A Novel. Post 8vo, illustrated boards, 2s.

Woolley (Celia Parker).—Rachel Armstrong; or, Love and Theology. Post 8vo, illustrated boards, 2s.; cloth, 2s. 6d.

Wright (Thomas), Works by. Crown 8vo, cloth extra, 7s. 6d. each.
The Caricature History of the Georges. With 400 Caricatures, Squibs, &c.
History of Caricature and of the Grotesque in Art, Literature, Sculpture, and Painting. Illustrated by F. W. FAIRHOLT, F.S.A.

Wynman (Margaret).—My Flirtations. With 13 Illustrations by J. BERNARD PARTRIDGE. Post 8vo, cloth, 3s. 6d.

Yates (Edmund), Novels by. Post 8vo, illustrated boards, 2s. each.
Land at Last. | The Forlorn Hope. | Castaway.

Zangwill (I.). — Ghetto Tragedies. With Three Illustrations by A. S. BOYD. Fcap. 8vo, picture cover, 1s. net.

Zola (Emile), Novels by. Crown 8vo, cloth extra, 3s. 6d. each.
The Fat and the Thin. Translated by ERNEST A. VIZETELLY.
Money. Translated by ERNEST A. VIZETELLY.
The Downfall. Translated by E. A. VIZETELLY.
The Dream. Translated by ELIZA CHASE. With Eight Illustrations by JEANNIOT.
Doctor Pascal. Translated by E. A. VIZETELLY. With Portrait of the Author.
Lourdes. Translated by ERNEST A. VIZETELLY.
Rome. Translated by ERNEST A. VIZETELLY. [Shortly.

SOME BOOKS CLASSIFIED IN SERIES.

. For fuller cataloguing, see alphabetical arrangement, pp. 1-26.

The Mayfair Library. Post 8vo, cloth limp, 2s. 6d. per Volume.

A Journey Round My Room. By X. DE MAISTRE. Translated by Sir HENRY ATTWELL.
Quips and Quiddities. By W. D. ADAMS.
The Agony Column of 'The Times.'
Melancholy Anatomised: Abridgment of BURTON.
Poetical Ingenuities. By W. T. DOBSON.
The Cupboard Papers. By FIN-BEC.
W. S. Gilbert's Plays. Three Series.
Songs of Irish Wit and Humour.
Animals and their Masters. By Sir A. HELPS.
Social Pressure. By Sir A. HELPS.
Curiosities of Criticism. By H. J. JENNINGS.
The Autocrat of the Breakfast-Table. By OLIVER WENDELL HOLMES.
Pencil and Palette. By R. KEMPT.
Little Essays: from LAMB'S LETTERS.
Forensic Anecdotes. By JACOB LARWOOD.

Theatrical Anecdotes. By JACOB LARWOOD.
Jeux d'Esprit. Edited by HENRY S. LEIGH.
Witch Stories. By E. LYNN LINTON.
Ourselves. By E. LYNN LINTON.
Pastimes and Players. By R. MACGREGOR.
New Paul and Virginia. By W. H. MALLOCK.
The New Republic. By W. H. MALLOCK.
Puck on Pegasus. By H. C. PENNELL.
Pegasus Re-saddled. By H. C. PENNELL.
Muses of Mayfair. Edited by H. C. PENNELL.
Thoreau: His Life and Aims. By H. A. PAGE.
Puniana. By Hon. HUGH ROWLEY.
More Puniana. By Hon. HUGH ROWLEY.
The Philosophy of Handwriting.
By Stream and Sea. By WILLIAM SENIOR.
Leaves from a Naturalist's Note-Book. By Dr. ANDREW WILSON.

The Golden Library. Post 8vo, cloth limp, 2s. per Volume.

Diversions of the Echo Club. BAYARD TAYLOR.
Songs for Sailors. By W. C. BENNETT.
Lives of the Necromancers. By W. GODWIN.
The Poetical Works of Alexander Pope.
Scenes of Country Life. By EDWARD JESSE.
Tale for a Chimney Corner. By LEIGH HUNT.

The Autocrat of the Breakfast Table. By OLIVER WENDELL HOLMES.
La Mort d'Arthur: Selections from MALLORY.
Provincial Letters of Blaise Pascal.
Maxims and Reflections of Rochefoucauld.

The Wanderer's Library. Crown 8vo, cloth extra, 3s. 6d. each.

Wanderings in Patagonia. By JULIUS BEER-BOHM. Illustrated.
Merrie England in the Olden Time. By G. DANIEL. Illustrated by ROBERT CRUIKSHANK.
Circus Life. By THOMAS FROST.
Lives of the Conjurers. By THOMAS FROST.
The Old Showmen and the Old London Fairs. By THOMAS FROST.
Low-Life Deeps. By JAMES GREENWOOD.
The Wilds of London. By JAMES GREENWOOD.

Tunis. By Chev. HESSE-WARTEGG. 22 Illusts.
Life and Adventures of a Cheap Jack.
World Behind the Scenes. By P. FITZGERALD.
Tavern Anecdotes and Sayings.
The Genial Showman. By E. P. HINGSTON.
Story of London Parks. By JACOB LARWOOD.
London Characters. By HENRY MAYHEW.
Seven Generations of Executioners.
Summer Cruising in the South Seas. By C. WARREN STODDARD. Illustrated.

Books in Series—*continued.*

Handy Novels. Fcap. 8vo, cloth boards, 1s. 6d. each.

The Old Maid's Sweetheart. By A. St. Aubyn.
Modest Little Sara. By Alan St. Aubyn.
Seven Sleepers of Ephesus. M. E. Coleridge.
Taken from the Enemy. By H. Newbolt.

A Lost Soul. By W. L. Alden.
Dr. Palliser's Patient. By Grant Allen.
Monte Carlo Stories. By Joan Barrett.
Black Spirits and White. By R. A. Cram.

My Library. Printed on laid paper, post 8vo, half-Roxburghe, 2s. 6d. each.

Citation and Examination of William Shakspeare.
By W. S. Landor.
The Journal of Maurice de Guerin.

Christie Johnstone. By Charles Reade.
Peg Woffington. By Charles Reade.
The Dramatic Essays of Charles Lamb.

The Pocket Library. Post 8vo, printed on laid paper and hf.-bd., 2s. each.

The Essays of Elia. By Charles Lamb.
Robinson Crusoe. Illustrated by G. Cruikshank.
Whims and Oddities. By Thomas Hood.
The Barber's Chair. By Douglas Jerrold.
Gastronomy. By Brillat-Savarin.
The Epicurean, &c. By Thomas Moore.
Leigh Hunt's Essays. Edited by E. Ollier.

White's Natural History of Selborne.
Gulliver's Travels, &c. By Dean Swift.
Plays by Richard Brinsley Sheridan.
Anecdotes of the Clergy. By Jacob Larwood.
Thomson's Seasons. Illustrated.
Autocrat of the Breakfast-Table and The Professor
at the Breakfast-Table. By O. W. Holmes.

THE PICCADILLY NOVELS.

Library Editions of Novels, many Illustrated, crown 8vo, cloth extra, 3s. 6d. each.

By F. M. ALLEN.
Green as Grass.

By GRANT ALLEN.
Philistia.
Strange Stories.
Babylon.
For Maimie's Sake.
In all Shades.
The Beckoning Hand.
The Devil's Die.
This Mortal Coil.
The Tents of Shem.

The Great Taboo.
Dumaresq's Daughter.
Duchess of Powysland.
Blood Royal.
Ivan Greet's Masterpiece.
The Scallywag.
At Market Value.
Under Sealed Orders.

By MARY ANDERSON.
Othello's Occupation.

By EDWIN L. ARNOLD.
Phra the Phœnician. | Constable of St. Nicholas.

By ROBERT BARR.
In a Steamer Chair. | From Whose Bourne.

By FRANK BARRETT.
The Woman of the Iron Bracelets.

By 'BELLE.'
Vashti and Esther.

By Sir W. BESANT and J. RICE.
Ready-Money Mortiboy.
My Little Girl.
With Harp and Crown.
This Son of Vulcan.
The Golden Butterfly.
The Monks of Thelema.

By Celia's Arbour.
Chaplain of the Fleet.
The Seamy Side.
The Case of Mr. Lucraft.
In Trafalgar's Bay.
The Ten Years' Tenant.

By Sir WALTER BESANT.
All Sorts and Conditions of Men.
The Captains' Room.
All in a Garden Fair.
Dorothy Forster.
Uncle Jack.
The World Went Very Well Then.
Children of Gibeon.
Herr Paulus.
For Faith and Freedom.

To Call Her Mine.
The Bell of St. Paul's.
The Holy Rose.
Armorel of Lyonesse.
S. Katherine's by Tower
Verbena Camellia Stephanotis.
The Ivory Gate.
The Rebel Queen.
Beyond the Dreams of Avarice.

By PAUL BOURGET.
A Living Lie.

By ROBERT BUCHANAN.
Shadow of the Sword.
A Child of Nature.
God and the Man.
Martyrdom of Madeline.
Love Me for Ever.
Annan Water.
Foxglove Manor.

The New Abelard.
Matt. | Rachel Dene.
Master of the Mine.
The Heir of Linne.
Woman and the Man.
Red and White Heather.

ROB. BUCHANAN & HY. MURRAY.
The Charlatan.

By J. MITCHELL CHAPPLE.
The Minor Chord.

By HALL CAINE.
The Shadow of a Crime. | The Deemster.
A Son of Hagar.

By MACLAREN COBBAN.
The Red Sultan. | The Burden of Isabel.

By MORT. & FRANCES COLLINS.
Transmigration.
Blacksmith & Scholar.
The Village Comedy.

From Midnight to Midnight.
You Play me False.

By WILKIE COLLINS.
Armadale. | AfterDark.
No Name.
Antonina.
Basil.
Hide and Seek.
The Dead Secret.
Queen of Hearts.
My Miscellanies.
The Woman in White.
The Moonstone.
Man and Wife.
Poor Miss Finch.
Miss or Mrs. ?
The New Magdalen.

The Frozen Deep.
The Two Destinies.
The Law and the Lady.
The Haunted Hotel.
The Fallen Leaves.
Jezebel's Daughter.
The Black Robe.
Heart and Science.
'I Say No.'
Little Novels.
The Evil Genius.
The Legacy of Cain.
A Rogue's Life.
Blind Love.

By DUTTON COOK.
Paul Foster's Daughter.

By E. H. COOPER.
Geoffory Hamilton.

By V. CECIL COTES.
Two Girls on a Barge.

By C. EGBERT CRADDOCK.
His Vanished Star.

By H. N. CRELLIN.
Romances of the Old Seraglio.

By MATT CRIM.
The Adventures of a Fair Rebel.

By S. R. CROCKETT and others.
Tales of Our Coast.

By B. M. CROKER.
Diana Barrington.
Proper Pride.
A Family Likeness.
Pretty Miss Neville.
A Bird of Passage.

'To Let.'
Mr. Jervis.
Village Tales & Jungle Tragedies.
The Real Lady Hilda.

By WILLIAM CYPLES.
Hearts of Gold.

By ALPHONSE DAUDET.
The Evangelist ; or, Port Salvation.

By H. COLEMAN DAVIDSON.
Mr. Sadler's Daughters.

By ERASMUS DAWSON.
The Fountain of Youth.

By JAMES DE MILLE.
A Castle in Spain.

THE PICCADILLY (3/6) NOVELS—*continued.*

By J. LEITH DERWENT.

Our Lady of Tears. | Circe's Lovers.

By DICK DONOVAN.

Tracked to Doom. | The Mystery of Jamaica
Man from Manchester. | Terrace.

By A. CONAN DOYLE.

The Firm of Girdlestone.

By S. JEANNETTE DUNCAN.

A Daughter of To-day. | Vernon's Aunt.

By G. MANVILLE FENN.

The New Mistress. | The Tiger Lily.
Witness to the Deed. | The White Virgin.

By PERCY FITZGERALD.

Fatal Zero.

By R. E. FRANCILLON.

One by One. | Ropes of Sand.
A Dog and his Shadow. | Jack Doyle's Daughter.
A Real Queen. |

Prefaced by Sir BARTLE FRERE.

Pandurang Hari.

BY EDWARD GARRETT.

The Capel Girls.

By PAUL GAULOT.

The Red Shirts.

By CHARLES GIBBON.

Robin Gray. | The Golden Shaft.
Loving a Dream. |

By E. GLANVILLE.

The Lost Heiress. | The Fossicker.
A Fair Colonist. | The Golden Rock.

By E. J. GOODMAN.

The Fate of Herbert Wayne.

By Rev. S. BARING GOULD.

Red Spider. | Eve.

By CECIL GRIFFITH.

Corinthia Marazion.

By SYDNEY GRUNDY.

The Days of his Vanity.

By THOMAS HARDY.

Under the Greenwood Tree.

By BRET HARTE.

A Waif of the Plains. | Susy.
A Ward of the Golden | Sally Dows.
Gate. | A Protégée of Jack
A Sappho of Green | Hamlin's.
Springs. | Bell-Ringer of Angel's.
Col. Starbottle's Client. | Clarence.

By JULIAN HAWTHORNE.

Garth. | Beatrix Randolph.
Ellice Quentin. | David Poindexter's Dis-
Sebastian Strome. | appearance.
Dust. | The Spectre of the
Fortune's Fool. | Camera.

By Sir A. HELPS.

Ivan de Biron.

By I. HENDERSON.

Agatha Page.

By G. A. HENTY.

Rujub the Juggler. | Dorothy's Double.

By JOHN HILL.

The Common Ancestor.

By Mrs. HUNGERFORD.

Lady Verner's Flight. | The Three Graces.
The Red-House Mystery. |

By Mrs. ALFRED HUNT.

The Leaden Casket. | Self-Condemned.
That Other Person. | Mrs. Juliet.

By C. J. CUTCLIFFE HYNE.

Honour of Thieves.

By R. ASHE KING.

A Drawn Game.
'The Wearing of the Green.'

By EDMOND LEPELLETIER.

Madame Sans-Gène.

By HARRY LINDSAY.

Rhoda Roberts.

By E. LYNN LINTON.

Patricia Kemball. | Sowing the Wind.
Under which Lord? | The Atonement of Leam
'My Love!' | Dundas.
Ione. | The World Well Lost.
Paston Carew. | The One Too Many.

By HENRY W. LUCY.

Gideon Fleyce.

By JUSTIN McCARTHY.

A Fair Saxon. | Miss Misanthrope.
Linley Rochford. | Donna Quixote.
Dear Lady Disdain. | Red Diamonds.
Camiola. | Maid of Athens.
Waterdale Neighbours. | The Dictator.
My Enemy's Daughter. | The Comet of a Season.

By JUSTIN H. McCARTHY.

A London Legend.

By GEORGE MACDONALD.

Heather and Snow. | Phantastes.

By L. T. MEADE.

A Soldier of Fortune. | In an Iron Grip.

By BERTRAM MITFORD.

The Gun-Runner. | The King's Assegai.
The Luck of Gerard | Renshaw Fanning's
Ridgeley. | Quest.

By J. E. MUDDOCK.

Maid Marian and Robin Hood.
Basile the Jester.

By D. CHRISTIE MURRAY.

A Life's Atonement. | First Person Singular.
Joseph's Coat. | Cynic Fortune.
Coals of Fire. | The Way of the World.
Old Blazer's Hero. | BobMartin's Little Girl.
Val Strange. | Hearts. | Time's Revenges.
A Model Father. | A Wasted Crime.
By the Gate of the Sea. | In Direst Peril.
A Bit of Human Nature. | Mount Despair.

By MURRAY and HERMAN.

The Bishops' Bible. | Paul Jones's Alias.
One Traveller Returns. |

By HUME NISBET.

'Ball Up!'

By W. E. NORRIS.

Saint Ann's. | Billy Bellew.

By G. OHNET.

A Weird Gift.

By OUIDA.

Held in Bondage. | Two Little Wooden
Strathmore. | Shoes.
Chandos. | In a Winter City.
Under Two Flags. | Friendship.
Idalia. | Moths.
Cecil Castlemaine's | Ruffino.
Gage. | Pipistrello.
Tricotrin. | A Village Commune.
Puck. | Bimbi.
Folle Farine. | Wanda.
A Dog of Flanders. | Frescoes. | Othmar.
Pascarel. | In Maremma.
Signa. | Syrlin. | Guilderoy.
Princess Napraxine. | Santa Barbara.
Ariadne. | Two Offenders.

By MARGARET A. PAUL.

Gentle and Simple.

By JAMES PAYN.

Lost Sir Massingberd. | High Spirits.
Less Black than We're | Under One Roof.
Painted. | Glow-worm Tales.
A Confidential Agent. | The Talk of the Town.
A Grape from a Thorn. | Holiday Tasks.
In Peril and Privation. | For Cash Only.
The Mystery of Mir- | The Burnt Million.
By Proxy. [bridge. | The Word and the Will.
The Canon's Ward. | Sunny Stories.
Walter's Word. | A Trying Patient.

THE PICCADILLY (3/6) NOVELS—*continued*.

By Mrs. CAMPBELL PRAED.
Outlaw and Lawmaker. | Christina Chard.

By E. C. PRICE.
Valentina. | Mrs. Lancaster's Rival.
The Foreigners.

By RICHARD PRYCE.
Miss Maxwell's Affections.

By CHARLES READE.
It is Never Too Late to Mend. | Singleheart and Double-face.
The Double Marriage. | Good Stories of Men and other Animals.
Love Me Little, Love Me Long. | Hard Cash.
The Cloister and the Hearth. | Peg Woffington.
| Christie Johnstone.
The Course of True Love. | Griffith Gaunt.
| Foul Play.
The Autobiography of a Thief. | The Wandering Heir.
| A Woman-Hater.
Put Yourself in His Place. | A Simpleton.
| A Perilous Secret.
A Terrible Temptation. | Readiana.
The Jilt.

By Mrs. J. H. RIDDELL.
Weird Stories.

By AMELIE RIVES.
Barbara Dering.

By F. W. ROBINSON.
The Hands of Justice.

By DORA RUSSELL.
A Country Sweetheart. | The Drift of Fate.

By W. CLARK RUSSELL.
Ocean Tragedy. | Is He the Man?
My Shipmate Louise. | The Good Ship 'Mohock.'
Alone on Wide Wide Sea |
The Phantom Death. | The Convict Ship.

By JOHN SAUNDERS.
Guy Waterman. | The Two Dreamers.
Bound to the Wheel. | The Lion in the Path.

By KATHARINE SAUNDERS.
Margaret and Elizabeth | Heart Salvage.
Gideon's Rock. | Sebastian.
The High Mills.

By ADELINE SERGEANT.
Dr. Endicott's Experiment.

By HAWLEY SMART.
Without Love or Licence.

By T. W. SPEIGHT.
A Secret of the Sea. | The Grey Monk.

By ALAN ST. AUBYN.
A Fellow of Trinity. | In Face of the World.
The Junior Dean. | Orchard Damerel.
Master of St. Benedict's. | The Tremlett Diamonds
To his Own Master.

By JOHN STAFFORD.
Doris and I.

By R. A. STERNDALE.
The Afghan Knife.

By BERTHA THOMAS.
Proud Maisie. | The Violin-Player.

By ANTHONY TROLLOPE.
The Way we Live Now. | Scarborough's Family.
Frau Frohmann. | The Land-Leaguers.

By FRANCES E. TROLLOPE.
Like Ships upon the Sea. | Anne Furness.
| Mabel's Progress.

By IVAN TURGENIEFF, &c.
Stories from Foreign Novelists.

By MARK TWAIN.
The American Claimant. | Pudd'nhead Wilson.
The £1,000,000 Bank-note. | Tom Sawyer, Detective.
Tom Sawyer Abroad.

By C. C. FRASER-TYTLER.
Mistress Judith.

By SARAH TYTLER.
Lady Bell. | The Blackhall Ghosts.
Buried Diamonds. | The Macdonald Lass.

By ALLEN UPWARD.
The Queen against Owen.
The Prince of Balkistan.

By E. A. VIZETELLY.
The Scorpion: A Romance of Spain.

By ATHA WESTBURY.
The Shadow of Hilton Fernbrook.

By JOHN STRANGE WINTER.
A Soldier's Children.

By MARGARET WYNMAN.
My Flirtations.

By E. ZOLA.
The Downfall. | Money. | Lourdes.
The Dream. | The Fat and the Thin.
Dr. Pascal. | Rome.

CHEAP EDITIONS OF POPULAR NOVELS.
Post 8vo, illustrated boards, 2s. each.

By ARTEMUS WARD.
Artemus Ward Complete.

By EDMOND ABOUT.
The Fellah.

By HAMILTON AÏDÉ.
Carr of Carrlyon. | Confidences.

By MARY ALBERT.
Brooke Finchley's Daughter.

By Mrs. ALEXANDER.
Maid, Wife or Widow? | Valerie's Fate.

By GRANT ALLEN.
Philistia. | The Great Taboo.
Strange Stories. | Dumaresq's Daughter.
Babylon. | Duchess of Powysland.
For Maimie's Sake. | Blood Royal.
In all Shades. | Ivan Greet's Masterpiece.
The Beckoning Hand. |
The Devil's Die. | The Scallywag.
The Tents of Shem. | This Mortal Coil.

By E. LESTER ARNOLD.
Phra the Phœnician.

By SHELSLEY BEAUCHAMP.
Grantley Grange.

BY FRANK BARRETT.
Fettered for Life. | A Prodigal's Progress.
Little Lady Linton. | Found Guilty.
Between Life & Death. | A Recoiling Vengeance.
The Sin of Olga Zassoulich. | For Love and Honour.
| John Ford; and His Helpmate.
Folly Morrison. |
Lieut. Barnabas. | The Woman of the Iron Bracelets.
Honest Davie. |

By Sir W. BESANT and J. RICE.
Ready-Money Mortiboy | By Celia's Arbour.
My Little Girl. | Chaplain of the Fleet.
With Harp and Crown. | The Seamy Side.
This Son of Vulcan. | The Case of Mr. Lucraft.
The Golden Butterfly. | In Trafalgar's Bay.
The Monks of Thelema. | The Ten Years' Tenant.

By Sir WALTER BESANT.
All Sorts and Conditions of Men. | For Faith and Freedom.
| To Call Her Mine.
The Captains' Room. | The Bell of St. Paul's.
All in a Garden Fair. | The Holy Rose.
Dorothy Forster. | Armorel of Lyonesse.
Uncle Jack. | S. Katherine's by Tower.
The World Went Very Well Then. | Verbena Camellia Stephanotis.
Children of Gibeon. | The Ivory Gate.
Herr Paulus. | The Rebel Queen.

By AMBROSE BIERCE.
In the Midst of Life.

TWO-SHILLING NOVELS—*continued.*

By FREDERICK BOYLE.
Camp Notes. | Chronicles of No-man's
Savage Life. | Land.

BY BRET HARTE.
Californian Stories. | Flip. | Maruja.
Gabriel Conroy. | A Phyllis of the Sierras.
The Luck of Roaring | A Waif of the Plains.
   Camp. | A Ward of the Golden
An Heiress of Red Dog. | Gate.

By HAROLD BRYDGES.
Uncle Sam at Home.

By ROBERT BUCHANAN.
Shadow of the Sword. | The Martyrdom of Ma-
A Child of Nature. | deline.
God and the Man. | The New Abelard.
Love Me for Ever. | Matt.
Foxglove Manor. | The Heir of Linne.
The Master of the Mine. | Woman and the Man.
Annan Water.

By HALL CAINE.
The Shadow of a Crime. | The Deemster.
A Son of Hagar.

By Commander CAMERON.
The Cruise of the 'Black Prince.'

By Mrs. LOVETT CAMERON.
Deceivers Ever. | Juliet's Guardian.

By HAYDEN CARRUTH.
The Adventures of Jones.

By AUSTIN CLARE.
For the Love of a Lass.

By Mrs. ARCHER CLIVE.
Paul Ferroll.
Why Paul Ferroll Killed his Wife.

By MACLAREN COBBAN.
The Cure of Souls. | The Red Sultan.

By C. ALLSTON COLLINS.
The Bar Sinister.

By MORT. & FRANCES COLLINS.
Sweet Anne Page. | Sweet and Twenty.
Transmigration. | The Village Comedy.
From Midnight to Mid- | You Play me False.
   night. | Blacksmith and Scholar
A Fight with Fortune. | Frances.

By WILKIE COLLINS.
Armadale. | After Dark. | My Miscellanies.
No Name. | The Woman in White.
Antonina. | The Moonstone.
Basil. | Man and Wife.
Hide and Seek. | Poor Miss Finch.
The Dead Secret. | The Fallen Leaves.
Queen of Hearts. | Jezebel's Daughter.
Miss or Mrs.? | The Black Robe.
The New Magdalen. | Heart and Science.
The Frozen Deep. | 'I Say No!'
The Law and the Lady | The Evil Genius.
The Two Destinies. | Little Novels.
The Haunted Hotel. | Legacy of Cain.
A Rogue's Life. | Blind Love.

By M. J. COLQUHOUN.
Every Inch a Soldier.

By DUTTON COOK.
Leo. | Paul Foster's Daughter.

By C. EGBERT CRADDOCK.
The Prophet of the Great Smoky Mountains.

By MATT CRIM.
The Adventures of a Fair Rebel.

By B. M. CROKER.
Pretty Miss Neville. | Proper Pride.
Diana Barrington. | A Family Likeness.
'To Let.' | Village Tales and Jungle
A Bird of Passage. | Tragedies.

By W. CYPLES.
Hearts of Gold.

By ALPHONSE DAUDET.
The Evangelist: or, Port Salvation.

By ERASMUS DAWSON.
The Fountain of Youth.

By JAMES DE MILLE.
A Castle in Spain.

By J. LEITH DERWENT.
Our Lady of Tears. | Circe's Lovers.

By CHARLES DICKENS.
Sketches by Boz. | Nicholas Nickleby.
Oliver Twist.

By DICK DONOVAN.
The Man-Hunter. | In the Grip of the Law.
Tracked and Taken. | From Information Re-
Caught at Last! | ceived.
Wanted! | Tracked to Doom.
Who Poisoned Hetty | Link by Link
   Duncan? | Suspicion Aroused.
Man from Manchester. | Dark Deeds.
A Detective's Triumphs | Riddles Read.

By Mrs. ANNIE EDWARDES.
A Point of Honour. | Archie Lovell.

By M. BETHAM-EDWARDS.
Felicia. | Kitty.

By EDWARD EGGLESTON.
Roxy.

By G. MANVILLE FENN.
The New Mistress. | The Tiger Lily.
Witness to the Deed.

By PERCY FITZGERALD.
Bella Donna. | Second Mrs. Tillotson.
Never Forgotten. | Seventy - five Brooke
Polly. | Street.
Fatal Zero. | The Lady of Brantome.

By P. FITZGERALD and others.
Strange Secrets.

By ALBANY DE FONBLANQUE.
Filthy Lucre.

By R. E. FRANCILLON.
Olympia. | King or Knave?
One by One. | Romances of the Law.
A Real Queen. | Ropes of Sand.
Queen Cophetua. | A Dog and his Shadow.

By HAROLD FREDERIC.
Seth's Brother's Wife. | The Lawton Girl.

Prefaced by Sir BARTLE FRERE.
Pandurang Hari.

By HAIN FRISWELL.
One of Two.

By EDWARD GARRETT.
The Capel Girls.

By GILBERT GAUL.
A Strange Manuscript.

By CHARLES GIBBON.
Robin Gray. | In Honour Bound.
Fancy Free. | Flower of the Forest.
For Lack of Gold. | The Braes of Yarrow.
What will World Say? | The Golden Shaft.
In Love and War. | Of High Degree.
For the King. | By Mead and Stream.
In Pastures Green. | Loving a Dream.
Queen of the Meadow. | A Hard Knot.
A Heart's Problem. | Heart's Delight.
The Dead Heart. | Blood-Money.

By WILLIAM GILBERT.
Dr. Austin's Guests. | The Wizard of the
James Duke. | Mountain.

By ERNEST GLANVILLE.
The Lost Heiress. | The Fossicker.
A Fair Colonist.

By Rev. S. BARING GOULD.
Red Spider. | Eve.

By HENRY GREVILLE.
A Noble Woman. | Nikanor.

By CECIL GRIFFITH.
Corinthia Marazion.

By SYDNEY GRUNDY.
The Days of his Vanity.

By JOHN HABBERTON.
Brueton's Bayou. | Country Luck.

By ANDREW HALLIDAY.
Every-day Papers.

By Lady DUFFUS HARDY.
Paul Wynter's Sacrifice.

Two-Shilling Novels—continued.

By THOMAS HARDY.
Under the Greenwood Tree.

By J. BERWICK HARWOOD.
The Tenth Earl.

By JULIAN HAWTHORNE.

Garth.	Beatrix Randolph.
Ellice Quentin.	Love—or a Name.
Fortune's Fool.	David Poindexter's Dis-
Miss Cadogna.	appearance.
Sebastian Strome.	The Spectre of the
Dust.	Camera.

By Sir ARTHUR HELPS.
Ivan de Biron.

By G. A. HENTY.
Rujub the Juggler.

By HENRY HERMAN.
A Leading Lady.

By HEADON HILL.
Zambra the Detective.

By JOHN HILL.
Treason Felony.

By Mrs. CASHEL HOEY.
The Lover's Creed.

By Mrs. GEORGE HOOPER.
The House of Raby.

By TIGHE HOPKINS.
Twixt Love and Duty.

By Mrs. HUNGERFORD.

A Maiden all Forlorn.	A Modern Circe.
In Durance Vile.	Lady Verner's Flight.
Marvel.	The Red House Mystery
A Mental Struggle.	

By Mrs. ALFRED HUNT.

Thornicroft's Model.	Self-Condemned.
That Other Person.	The Leaden Casket.

By JEAN INGELOW.
Fated to be Free.

By WM. JAMESON.
My Dead Self.

By HARRIETT JAY.
The Dark Colleen. | Queen of Connaught.

By MARK KERSHAW.
Colonial Facts and Fictions.

By R. ASHE KING.

A Drawn Game.	Passion's Slave.
'The Wearing of the	Bell Barry.
Green.'	

By JOHN LEYS.
The Lindsays.

By E. LYNN LINTON.

Patricia Kemball.	The Atonement of Leam
The World Well Lost.	Dundas.
Under which Lord?	With a Silken Thread.
Paston Carew.	Rebel of the Family.
'My Love!'	Sowing the Wind.
Ione.	The One Too Many.

By HENRY W. LUCY.
Gideon Fleyce.

By JUSTIN McCARTHY.

Dear Lady Disdain.	Camiola.
Waterdale Neighbours.	Donna Quixote.
My Enemy's Daughter.	Maid of Athens.
A Fair Saxon.	The Comet of a Season.
Linley Rochford.	The Dictator.
Miss Misanthrope.	Red Diamonds.

By HUGH MACCOLL.
Mr. Stranger's Sealed Packet.

By GEORGE MACDONALD.
Heather and Snow.

By AGNES MACDONELL.
Quaker Cousins.

By KATHARINE S. MACQUOID.
The Evil Eye. | Lost Rose.

By W. H. MALLOCK.
A Romance of the Nine- | The New Republic.
teenth Century.

By FLORENCE MARRYAT.

Open! Sesame!	A Harvest of Wild Oats.
Fighting the Air.	Written in Fire.

By J. MASTERMAN.
Half-a-dozen Daughters.

By BRANDER MATTHEWS.
A Secret of the Sea.

By L. T. MEADE.
A Soldier of Fortune.

By LEONARD MERRICK.
The Man who was Good.

By JEAN MIDDLEMASS.
Touch and Go. | Mr. Dorillion.

By Mrs. MOLESWORTH.
Hathercourt Rectory.

By J. E. MUDDOCK.

Stories Weird and Won-	From the Bosom of the
derful.	Deep.
The Dead Man's Secret.	

By D. CHRISTIE MURRAY.

A Model Father.	A Life's Atonement.
Joseph's Coat.	By the Gate of the Sea.
Coals of Fire.	A Bit of Human Nature.
Val Strange.	First Person Singular.
Old Blazer's Hero.	Bob Martin's Little Girl
Hearts.	Time's Revenges.
The Way of the World.	A Wasted Crime.
Cynic Fortune.	In Direst Peril.

By MURRAY and HERMAN.

One Traveller Returns.	The Bishops' Bible.
Paul Jones's Alias.	

By HENRY MURRAY.
A Game of Bluff. | A Song of Sixpence.

By HUME NISBET.
'Bail Up!' | Dr. Bernard St. Vincent.

By ALICE O'HANLON.
The Unforeseen. | Chance? or Fate?

By GEORGES OHNET.

Dr. Rameau.	A Weird Gift.
A Last Love.	

By Mrs. OLIPHANT.

Whiteladies.	The Greatest Heiress in
The Primrose Path.	England.

By Mrs. ROBERT O'REILLY.
Phœbe's Fortunes.

By OUIDA.

Held in Bondage.	Two Lit. Wooden Shoes.
Strathmore.	Moths.
Chandos.	Bimbi.
Idalia.	Pipistrello.
Under Two Flags.	A Village Commune.
Cecil Castlemaine's Gage	Wanda.
Tricotrin.	Othmar.
Puck.	Frescoes.
Folle Farine.	In Maremma.
A Dog of Flanders.	Guilderoy.
Pascarel.	Ruffino.
Signa.	Syrlin.
Princess Napraxine.	Santa Barbara.
In a Winter City.	Two Offenders.
Ariadne.	Ouida's Wisdom, Wit,
Friendship.	and Pathos.

By MARGARET AGNES PAUL
Gentle and Simple.

By C. L. PIRKIS.
Lady Lovelace.

By EDGAR A. POE.
The Mystery of Marie Roget.

By Mrs. CAMPBELL PRAED
The Romance of a Station.
The Soul of Countess Adrian.
Outlaw and Lawmaker.
Christina Chard.

By E. C. PRICE.

Valentina.	Mrs. Lancaster's Rival.
The Foreigners.	Gerald.

By RICHARD PRYCE.
Miss Maxwell's Affections.

TWO-SHILLING NOVELS—continued.

By JAMES PAYN.

Bentinck's Tutor.	The Talk of the Town.
Murphy's Master.	Holiday Tasks.
A County Family.	A Perfect Treasure.
At Her Mercy.	What He Cost Her.
Cecil's Tryst.	A Confidential Agent.
The Clyffards of Clyffe.	Glow-worm Tales.
The Foster Brothers.	The Burnt Million.
Found Dead.	Sunny Stories.
The Best of Husbands.	Lost Sir Massingberd.
Walter's Word.	A Woman's Vengeance.
Halves.	The Family Scapegrace.
Fallen Fortunes.	Gwendoline's Harvest.
Humorous Stories.	Like Father, Like Son.
£200 Reward.	Married Beneath Him.
A Marine Residence.	Not Wooed, but Won.
Mirk Abbey.	Less Black than We're
By Proxy.	Painted.
Under One Roof.	Some Private Views.
High Spirits.	A Grape from a Thorn.
Carlyon's Year.	The Mystery of Mir-
From Exile.	bridge.
For Cash Only.	The Word and the Will.
Kit.	A Prince of the Blood.
The Canon's Ward.	A Trying Patient.

By CHARLES READE.

It is Never Too Late to	A Terrible Temptation.
Mend.	Foul Play.
Christie Johnstone.	The Wandering Heir.
The Double Marriage.	Hard Cash.
Put Yourself in His	Singleheart and Double-
Place	face.
Love Me Little, Love	Good Stories of Men and
Me Long.	other Animals.
The Cloister and the	Peg Woffington.
Hearth.	Griffith Gaunt.
The Course of True	A Perilous Secret.
Love.	A Simpleton.
The Jilt.	Readiana.
The Autobiography of	A Woman-Hater.
a Thief.	

By Mrs. J. H. RIDDELL.

Weird Stories.	The Uninhabited House.
Fairy Water.	The Mystery in Palace.
Her Mother's Darling.	Gardens.
The Prince of Wales's	The Nun's Curse.
Garden Party.	Idle Tales.

By AMELIE RIVES.
Barbara Dering.

By F. W. ROBINSON.
Women are Strange. | The Hands of Justice.

By JAMES RUNCIMAN.
Skippers and Shellbacks. | Schools and Scholars.
Grace Balmaign's Sweetheart.

By W. CLARK RUSSELL.

Round the Galley Fire.	The Romance of Jenny
On the Fo'k'sle Head.	Harlowe.
In the Middle Watch.	An Ocean Tragedy.
A Voyage to the Cape.	My Shipmate Louise.
A Book for the Ham-	Alone on a Wide Wide
mock.	Sea.
The Mystery of the	
'Ocean Star.'	

By GEORGE AUGUSTUS SALA.
Gaslight and Daylight.

By JOHN SAUNDERS.
Guy Waterman. | The Lion in the Path.
The Two Dreamers.

By KATHARINE SAUNDERS.

Joan Merryweather.	Sebastian.
The High Mills.	Margaret and Eliza-
Heart Salvage.	beth.

By GEORGE R. SIMS.

Rogues and Vagabonds.	Tinkletop's Crime.
The Ring o' Bells.	Zeph.
Mary Jane's Memoirs.	My Two Wives.
Mary Jane Married.	Memoirs of a Landlady.
Tales of To-day.	Scenes from the Show.
Dramas of Life.	The 10 Commandments.

By ARTHUR SKETCHLEY.
Match in the Dark.

By HAWLEY SMART.
Without Love or Licence.

By T. W. SPEIGHT.

The Mysteries of Heron	Back to Life.
Dyke.	The Loudwater Tragedy.
The Golden Hoop.	Burgo's Romance.
Hoodwinked.	Quittance in Full.
By Devious Ways.	A Husband from the Sea.

By ALAN ST. AUBYN.

A Fellow of Trinity.	To His Own Master.
The Junior Dean.	Orchard Damerel.
Master of St. Benedict's	

By R. A. STERNDALE.
The Afghan Knife.

By R. LOUIS STEVENSON.
New Arabian Nights. | Prince Otto.

By BERTHA THOMAS.
Cressida. | The Violin-Player.
Proud Maisie.

By WALTER THORNBURY.
Tales for the Marines. | Old Stories Retold.

By T. ADOLPHUS TROLLOPE.
Diamond Cut Diamond.

By F. ELEANOR TROLLOPE.

Like Ships upon the	Anne Furness.
Sea.	Mabel's Progress.

By ANTHONY TROLLOPE.

Frau Frohmann.	The Land-Leaguers.
Marion Fay.	The American Senator.
Kept in the Dark.	Mr. Scarborough's
John Caldigate.	Family.
The Way We Live Now.	GoldenLion of Granpere

By J. T. TROWBRIDGE.
Farnell's Folly.

By IVAN TURGENIEFF, &c.
Stories from Foreign Novelists.

By MARK TWAIN.

A Pleasure Trip on the	Life on the Mississippi.
Continent.	The Prince and the
The Gilded Age.	Pauper.
Huckleberry Finn.	A Yankee at the Court
Mark Twain's Sketches.	of King Arthur.
Tom Sawyer.	The £1,000,000 Bank-
A Tramp Abroad.	Note.
Stolen White Elephant.	

By C. C. FRASER-TYTLER.
Mistress Judith.

By SARAH TYTLER.

The Bride's Pass.	The Huguenot Family.
Buried Diamonds.	The Blackhall Ghosts.
St. Mungo's City.	What She Came Through
Lady Bell.	Beauty and the Beast
Noblesse Oblige.	Citoyenne Jaqueline.
Disappeared.	

By ALLEN UPWARD.
The Queen against Owen.

By AARON WATSON and LILLIAS WASSERMANN.
The Marquis of Carabas.

By WILLIAM WESTALL.
Trust-Money.

By Mrs. F. H. WILLIAMSON.
A Child Widow.

By J. S. WINTER.
Cavalry Life. | Regimental Legends.

By H. F. WOOD.
The Passenger from Scotland Yard.
The Englishman of the Rue Cain.

By Lady WOOD.
Sabina.

By CELIA PARKER WOOLLEY.
Rachel Armstrong ; or, Love and Theology.

By EDMUND YATES.
The Forlorn Hope. | Castaway.
Land at Last.

OGDEN, SMALE AND CO., LIMITED, PRINTERS, GREAT SAFFRON HILL, E.C.

www.ingramcontent.com/pod-product-compliance
Lightning Source LLC
Chambersburg PA
CBHW030805020726
47499CB00006B/1773